Praise for Ker

"A soul-mate of Jim Thompson's, or maybe of James M. Cain's, he has a cast of characters which rates high on the deadbeat scale."
Irish Times

"Blurring different styles and genre traits is not only necessary for fiction to evolve and remain relevant, but it also makes for a damn exciting read ... Bruen's books are like odd architectural wonders, stark, strangely unsettling, beautifully classical, yet wholly modern."
Crime Factory

"Bruen is an original, grimly hilarious and gloriously Irish."
Patrick Anderson, *Washington Post*

Vixen

"The plot is exposed in a series of word explosions that reverberate on the page, a pace that kills, not for the faint-hearted but for those who like their crime novels down and dirty."
Vincent Banville, *Irish Times*

The Guards

"One of the most mesmerizing works of crime fiction I've ever read."
James W. Hall, author of *Off the Chart*

"An astounding novel, a poetic account of a desperation as deep and cold as the North Sea."
James Crumley, author of *The Final Country*

"I will henceforth be first in the queue for anything he writes."
Gene Kerrigan, *Sunday Independent*

The Magdalen Martyrs

"Bleak, unsettling and unmistakably original. Bruen seems to be alone in writing original Irish noir."

Martin Radcliff, *Time Out*

London Boulevard

"Truly great entertainment, permeated with a dark and disturbing strand that'll stay with you long after the final denouement. Treat yourselves."

David Peters, *Time Out*

"Low-life thugs, faded movie actresses and brainless killers illuminate the decaying gentility of Holland Park with systematic glee: clipped, breathless and addictive."

Maxim Jakubowski, *Guardian*

Her Last Call to Louis MacNeice

"The punchy, slangy, jokey narrative, rich in allusion to British and American popular culture, achieves an almost hypnotic quality."

Jon L. Breen, *Ellery Queen's Mystery Magazine*

White Trilogy

"Bruen bends the Irish tradition to his own ends and infuses it with the tensions of the thriller plot, a mix of black comedy and the ever present threat of violence that sets readers' teeth on edge. He strikes a perfect match between the edgy desperation of his characters and the city itself."

Dorothy Johnson, *Books Etc.*

"A very stylish writer. Violence, drugs, double-crosses and emotional betrayal all feature against a backdrop of sleazy London hotels and warehouses, and Bruen keeps the tension agonizingly high throughout. Very, very good."

Sunday Tribune

Ken Bruen was born in Galway in 1951. He spent twenty-five years as an English teacher in Africa, Japan, South-East Asia and South America. He has a PhD in metaphysics and has been shortlisted for the Edgar Awards 2004.

Dispatching Baudelaire

Dispatching Baudelaire

KEN BRUEN

First published 2004 by
SITRIC BOOKS
62–63 Sitric Road, Arbour Hill,
Dublin 7, Ireland
www.sitric.com

A CIP record for this title is available from The British Library.

1 3 5 7 9 10 8 6 4 2

ISBN 1 903305 12 8

Set in 12 on 16 pt Jensen
Printed by ColourBooks, Baldoyle, Dublin

For Roger Durham –
doctor, author, publisher and,
of course, rugby referee

Author's note

Baudelaire was written in the early nineties when London was still recovering from the Thatcher years: her shadow loomed large over the city. If you had to reach for a description of the spirit prevalent then, paranoia would fit best. The money-men in particular were jittery, still reeling from the crash of the eighties, and once you throw certain drugs into the mix, you get serious nerves. The price of cocaine had skyrocketed and money, well money was the prime motivator, as in most encounters.

White-collar crime was the topic of ferocious dinner parties. I wanted to explore what might happen to the "safe" professions if they were seduced by the usual suspects:

money,

sex,

power,

take an accountant and lure him down the meaner streets, see how he'd fare. I wanted to question how solid, how safe was the blandest of our citizens. Throw Baudelaire into the mesh and you'll tilt those scales in any era. There are few more dangerous animals than an Englishman off balance.

Ken Bruen

New York, January 2004

Dispatching Baudelaire

But after time
we soberly descend
a little newer
for the term
upon enchanted ground.

Emily D.

Book 1

"YOU HAVE A MEAN FUCKIN' MOUTH."

That's the very first thing she ever said to me. Nice, eh! And I don't, I mean, OK I tend to compress my lips a bit, but that doesn't make it mean. Not really. I do that to hide an over-bite. So sure, my teeth aren't the shine-in-the-dark model, but they're hardly green. But whoa, hold the phones, this makes me sound defensive ... and I've nothing to defend, but let's leave that for now.

Anyroads, as they say in *Coronation Street*, that's how I met her. In The Nell Gwynn off The Strand. It was chock-a-block in there. She'd squeezed in beside me at the bar and hey presto, she's bad-mouthing me, if you'll excuse the pun.

To describe her, as she was then, that very first moment, how she looked, not how she was, because she kept the two rigidly separate. She was small with jet black hair. Later I learnt she put darkener in it. Light blue eyes with fast intelligence. A snub nose and yes, a generous mouth, full lips and good teeth. Very thin and it seemed, no chest. Her skin was pale with a sheen of ... I don't know, it appeared to pick up the light. That sounds daft, but that's how it looked.

Sexy, yes. From the beginning, that was all over her. She wasn't even especially pretty, but some mix in there made you want to climb on, forever.

"You're not a policeman?"

"Good Lord, no."

"You have the eyes of one, dull and blatant. But you do have a name?"

I hesitated, not because I didn't want to tell her. I was fairly offended by the eyes remark. I'd always thought they were my one solid feature.

"How terribly English," she said, "you can't say as we haven't been properly introduced. Well, pardon me ... Yo, bar-person, double vodka before Tuesday."

"Mike," I said.

She gave a brief smile.

"Solid and reliable, Mike ... good old rigid Micky eh. You're not fibbing here and it's really Harry – yeah, you look like a Harry, dirty Harry."

Her drink came and she said,

"Give Harry another ... reason I ask if you're a policeman is I'm a bit wired, been doing the old nosy candy."

I had no trouble at all believing this and then she slapped the counter, saying,

"That shit costs, you know. Orson Welles liked it so much he said if he'd a spare lifetime to waste, he would give it to cocaine."

Is there an answer to this? Probably. But it wasn't one I could come up with. You know you're in deep trouble with a woman when you want to impress her. So I had some of my drink.

Now she inspected me. I'll try to tell you what I think she saw. Not what I hoped she'd see. I'm 5'10" with a medium build, brown straight hair, brown eyes, an ordinary nose and you already heard about the mouth. Neat, I look neat and alas, not in the American sense. The sort of baby they very nearly forgot to deliver. And did definitely forget after. Good Lord, you'd think I wanted to be tidy.

What a horror. On my gravestone it will say,

"He died tidy."

When they talk about the "public" I'm exactly who they see, however briefly. Christ, I'm verging on caricature.

"Mike ... yo, Mikey, earth calling?"

"Sorry."

"That is one black suit, how come you're in a pub after two – skiving off the job, eh?"

"My mother died."

She looked at me, not with concern or compassion, but with a sort of lazy interest. I mean she'd just met me, how torn up could she be about my mother?

"I'm sorry, Mike."

"Oh, don't be, that was five years ago."

"What? You're still taking time off? ... Jesus Mikey, time to get a grip. The firm's probably sold for fuckssake."

"No ... no, I only just told them. I kept her death quiet until now. I thought I'd keep it in reserve till I really wanted time off."

She took a lofty wallop of her drink and said,

"Weird, what? You stashed yer old Mum under the bed and then hauled her out when you wanted a bit of a holiday. You don't need cocaine, Mikey, it's lockin' up you need."

As I mentioned, the pub was packed and a stout man in a pin-stripe had been trying for service. He kicked against me and my drink spilled. She turned instantly, said,

"Hey, lard ass ... yeah, fat face, easy with the pushing."

"Are you addressing me, Miss?"

"Got stockings and suspenders on under the suit? ... Yes, you do. I know you, let's check it out."

She moved towards him. He looked to me, but I wasn't offering anything, least of all assistance. He pulled back and let the crowd help his escape.

I thought I'd go too and she asked,

"So, Mike, what work do you do?"

"I keep books."

"Yeah, but keep 'em where and for what? ... You're good with numbers, right?"

"Ahm, yes ... well, there's a little more to it."

"Try this number – 081-913-4897, you want a little freelance work, gimme a call."

And she was gone. In pursuit of the pinstripe, I dunno.

Everybody has a Laura story. This was the beginning of mine.

I had wanted to ask her what she did. I'd have guessed an actress. My mother used to say, "All women act – with men around, there's little option." As it was, I'd have guessed wrong.

MY FRIEND BRAD IS A HOMOSEXUAL.
He says,

"Hell is to have missed your life,"

and he gives me a very direct look – I've played safe. No risks and thus no excitement. Just kept my head down and hoped it would soon be over.

In a posh moment, I'd admitted to Brad that I only wanted to be safe. He said,

"Michael, that's not safety you're talking about."

"Yes it is."

"Man, you're talking dead. Ain't no real safety till death. Even then …

"And if you don't believe it," he'd said, "take a stroll down Oxford Street. Only Phil Collins believes in the cheery lovable scamp."

I'd asked what on earth Phil Collins had to do with it and got the reply,

"Or with anything else either!"

Brad is a teacher, a T.E.F.L., he says. Teacher of English as a Foreign Language. I've known him since childhood. We lived in the same street, went to the same schools. I'm not going to say obscene things like I've nothing against gays ... or worse, the ultimate insult, "Some of my best friends are gay." If you have to explain your friends, you aren't one.

I called round to see him that evening. K.D. Lang was blasting from his stereo. I had to wait till she finished.

"And so it shall be."

If I'd been seeking omens, might I not have listened to her. What I found instead was a lengthy song. Brad looks a bit like TAB HUNTER, and truth be told, he works at that. Why he should is a mystery. I always felt even Tab didn't want to look as he did.

Another long delay for real coffee to be made. A fuss with filters and clear water. Then I told him the Laura story. I omitted the mean-mouth detail lest he agree with the description.

"Michael, don't confuse crazy with interesting; she's a lunatic."

I was offended, but tried to hide it.

He said,

"You're offended, aren't you?"

"No, no, I value your insight."

"Michael, when people 'value your insight' they mean, 'Jeez, what did I ask this fucker for?'"

He turned up the volume on the stereo. Now K.D. was duetting with Roy Orbison for,

"Crying".

Brad joined them for the very high notes. I sipped on the real coffee and found it bitter.

So I rang her.

And I taped the call.

I didn't even know her name. I did instantly know her voice.

"Hello?"

"Yes … ahm, hello, I met you in a pub the other day … Good Lord, that sounds awful."

"Which, that you met me, or …"

"Oh no, I mean I was glad to meet you, to have made your acquaintance."

"Stop whining … OK, is there a point to this?"

"Yes … sorry … I … I wondered if I might take you to dinner, I'm … I …"

"The guy in the dead suit, yeah. I remember you want to get in my knickers, is that it?"

"I beg your pardon … That was not my intention … Good heavens, I don't even know your name."

"You don't want in my knickers? Is there something wrong with you – are you gay? … Is that it? … Speak up … I'm Laura. And you're Daniel if I remember correctly."

"Ahm … Mike actually."

"Mike, do I remember a Mike … well … wot the hell. This is Thursday."

"Actually it's Tuesday."

"Hey, Mike, lighten up … These are jokes – if there's correction to be done, I'll handle that … Are we clear?"

"So, meet me in that pub on Saturday at eight. That was on the Tottenham Court Road, am I correct?"

And she hung up.

I hadn't liked to say it was The Strand, but I worried about it. And worse, I was rampant.

I taped the call so I'd be able to hear that voice at my leisure. But I didn't think I'd be able to take my own pitiful effort.

What I did was, I played it for Brad.

After, he asked to hear it again. But before I could do that, he roared,

"Christ, I'm not serious, it's a movie cliché ... to pretend I'm interested or something. What do you want, Michael, you want me to tell you she's a little treasure, is that it?"

"I just wanted your opinion."

"She's a hooker."

"Thanks, Brad, thanks a lot. You'd know a lot about women after all."

I dunno if it hurt him. It was meant to.

He stood and said,

"You're right about that. I *do* know a lot about them. Last I heard, straight men didn't seem to have progressed much in their understanding of the female mind. But what about Brenda, eh, what about *HER*?"

There isn't a whole lot about Brenda. She's a nice person, in fact, she's a tidy one. There isn't a thing you could say against her. Or in fact, much you could say about her at all. Like me I suppose.

We'd been going together for two years, and going quietly. I know this sounds terrible, as if I hated her. After meeting Laura, I did think we were a match. Brenda was a secretary ... and sensible ... and sexless. When we went to bed, we thanked each other a lot. I dunno if that's consideration or just English.

Do you know the actress Rita Tushingham? Now I don't think she could be accused of being a beauty. Can you picture a plain version of her? That's pretty close to Brenda. I didn't *ever* tape her voice. I didn't want to hear her voice, even when I was with her.

A few months back, I'd gone on a shopping blitz. I dunno what possessed me, but instead of the usual dark jacket and slacks I'd buy twice yearly, I'd bought a pair of very faded jeans. The salesman kept calling me sir. The term loaded with a sneer.

"These are Levis 501. Sir will find them to be state of the art."

Art?

For jeans. Just holding them in my hands made me weak. I wanted to quip, "Who bought the other 500?" But when I tried them on, the old me surfaced and I asked, oh God –

"Will they hold a crease?"

He gave a tolerant chuckle.

"Oh, Sir, how droll, very humourous. The modern man doesn't iron his jeans. Creases are passé, oh dear me, yes."

I wondered if the modern man had a less modern woman for the ironing. I'd love to tell my boss about creases. Crease him right up.

So I bought the jeans … *and* trainers, and a beat-up leather jacket. I felt pretty beat up at the cost. The more bedraggled the clothes, the steeper the price. I'd obviously missed the revolution. Of course, I'd never worn them, good heavens no.

I wore them now. Brenda was already seated at our regular table at Pizza Hut. She was dressed as if at work. Her eyes widened.

"Michael, what on earth?"

"What do you think?"

"Well … it's different, I'll have to think about it."

The waitress came, smiled that pizza smile, and asked,

"The usual?"

"Yes," Brenda said.

"No," I said.

Brenda gave me a troubled look. I turned to the waitress. " Let us have our usual, but to go – can you do that?"

She could.

"Brenda, I have some nice wine at home, so let's break the routine and have a picnic on the floor, a bit of a lark."

"But, Michael, we're already out. I do wish you'd let me know. I'm not complaining, it's just … well."

"Yeah, you are, you are complaining."

"Oh, Michael, what's got into you, why are you determined to be disagreeable?"

I wanted to hit her.

We arrived back to my place in a cloud of knife politeness.

"After you, dear ..."

"No, no ... go along."

"Baby, I'm fine."

"Nothing's the matter ..."

"At least the rain held off."

Violence served through etiquette.

I own a semi-detached off Clapham Common. Inherited from my mother. It's

clean,
functional,
solid.

The only extravagance is my sound-system and my opera collection. Brenda clutched the pizza box like an accusation, said,

"I'll pop these in the microwave, darling, shall I?"

I had to bite down not to reply,

"And then I'll pop in you, how would that be, honeybunch?"

It hit me that just maybe Brenda couldn't abide me either. A perfect set of circumstances for marriage.

I lined up "Caro Nome" from *Rigoletto*. The beauty of Anna Moffo's voice rose and I increased the volume.

The chorus is conducted by Georg Solti and filled my ears. I could barely hear Brenda's voice,

"Is that Bizet, darling?"

"Verdi."

"A trifle loud, is it, darling?"

She was setting the microwave when I came up behind her. Her neat two-piece suit looking fresh from the dry-cleaners.

I put my arm around her neck and pushed myself against her. I began to kiss her neck.

"Not now darling, surely?"

I tightened my grip and pushed my other hand under her skirt. Tore at her tights and knickers. She tried to move, but I forced her against the oven. I pulled my zip down and rammed it into her. I came in seconds.

The microwave gave a "ping".

I pulled my arm away and staggered back to the living-room. I thought,

"The wine should be well chilled now, like the atmosphere."

BRAD WAS SAYING,

"I could kill for a fuckin' cigarette."

I thought, "Nice expression from an English language teacher."

I said nothing.

He continued,

"There isn't anything I haven't tried to stop: nicotine patches, acupuncture, hypnotherapy, aversion therapy."

I said, "Have you tried arithmetic?"

"Arithmetic ... wot, that a joke is it? Some form of fuckin' accountancy humour."

"No, it's figures – see how much it costs ... how many years ..."

"Fuck off, Mikey – just go the fuck home, OK? I even tried 'Quitman'. Heard of that, eh? It's electrocution ... yeah, I'm serious. It looks like a walkman and emits a tiny painless electric current behind the ears."

"You're serious, are you?"

"Yeah, the current activates a chemical reaction in the brain which reduces the horror of withdrawal."

"Did it work?"

"Fuck knows, the cost of it put me back smoking. That's nicotine logic Mike, don't try to follow it."

I wanted to talk to him about Laura. He asked,

"How's Brenda?"

And that I did not wish to discuss. In a loud voice he began to recite.

"Tobacco: divine, rare, super, excellent tobacco, a remedy to all diseases. But, as it is commonly abused by most men,

'tis a plague,

a mischief,

a violent surge of goods,

lands,

health,

and 'tis hellish,

devilish,

the ruin and overthrow of body and soul."

He stopped, reached in his pocket, took out a thin packet ... extracted one ... lit it and asked,

"Name the author ... Come along, quickly now."

I had no idea, so I said,

"I've no idea."

"Ah, take a shout, man, don't be a spineless shite all yer life."

"Sir Walter Raleigh then."

"Not bad, a touch of educated ignorance there."

Between us always hung an old betrayal. Never mentioned – or forgotten.

A time back, Brad's birthday, we'd gone out to dinner. My treat.

A few drinks after. The pub was in Kensington and catered to a wide range of tastes. Down the bar from us, three hard cases were loud and obvious. Brad was in his Oscar Wilde mode and broke off to address them.

"Oh, darlings ... Yo sweetmeats! Try and keep the volume down,"

and back to his Wilde stories. To my great relief, the three left soon after. Come closing, we were very drunk and very happy about it.

Outside, the three were waiting. One said,

"Hey, nancy boy ... Yeah, queer boy, arse-bandit, you want to tell us about that volume now?"

I ran.

All the adjectives

despicable,

unbelievable,

contemptuous,

apply.

No defence. I can't blame the booze as I was sober enough to run the fastest I've ever done ... and hail a taxi.

I put distance between us and they put Brad in hospital. When I went up to see him, he looked truly shocking, but his mouth still worked. He said,

"It's just a scratch, right?"

"Jesus."

I had a bunch of grapes and a box of Black Magic. They looked more pathetic than Brad. He glanced at them, said,

"Grapes of wrath, perchance. You should see the state of those other guys. They won't fuck with old Brad again."

"Oh God, Brad, I'm so sorry ... I ..."

"You ran for help ... That was it, Mike ... wasn't it?"

"I did, that's what I did –"

"Course it was, who'd desert their mate ... I mean, come on ..."

I needed the lie as badly as him. Else what? But it hung there a moment, washed over us and debased our friendship for life. Odd times, in the following months, I'd catch him looking at me. The expression wasn't disgust, but bafflement. Most of his injuries healed, but a slight limp was noticeable. In moments of madness, I could believe he'd developed it deliberately. It was effective. I felt that limp like amputation. He'd usually quip,

"Touch of the Lord Byron's, eh ... Do you think kids will call me names? 'Yo, Jimmy-the-gimp.'"

"I don't think they'd try it twice."

"What ... I could chase them, is that it? Wobble after them ... beat them with my VERBALS, that how you see it, Mikey?"

"I dunno."

"No, I don't think you do."

"GETTING FUCKED AND BEING OWNED are inseparably the same."

Laura's opening line to me. I'd arrived in an anxious state lest she wouldn't show. What she was showing was her legs. Not so much a short skirt as a loincloth. She added,

"Feast yer eyes, sucker."

I tried not to. She continued,

"Ever heard of McKinnon and Dworkin?"

"No."

"Why would you, you're a man."

I had no reply.

The barman hovered and Laura said,

"Couple of double whiskies, beer chasers."

Then to me,

"So, what alias do you wish to assume this evening?"

"Still Mike, I'm afraid."

She gave an unpleasant laugh, more a snigger.

"Wotcha afraid of, cock? Be Mike – live a little."

The drinks came. I reached for one.

"Yo, Mike, better pay the man first. I don't think he's treating us."

I opened my wallet. A monument to neatness. Everything lived in its financial place. A picture of a woman with a blond curly-haired child. Came with the wallet. I extracted a crisp, flat twenty. Brad reckons I iron my money. Not the worst idea I'd ever heard. As an accountant, I know about the laundering of cash.

The barman snapped it in jig time, bounced my change on the counter. Some coins only and precious few. Prices had taken a hike but not that much. There should be at least some folding stuff, if only for appearances. He gave a full smile, full of malice. So many teeth in his mouth, it had to hurt.

Laura gave me an expectant look.

I said,

"It seems a tad short!"

"I took one for myself, it's customary."

Laura grabbed his hand.

"It's also friggin' customary to be asked. Give him his money."

He put up his hands,

"Hey folks – just kidding around, OK?"

Laura said,

"Asshole."

I said nothing.

We moved to a table and she gave me a thorough examination, said,

"So, Mike, you've got balls after all. I had you pegged as a wimp."

I thought, "Don't tell Brad." I raised my glass, said,

"Here's looking at you, Laura."

"Don't talk shite – tell me something profound and tell me now."

"OK.

" 'If you make me your authority,' said the Master to a starry-eyed disciple, 'you harm yourself because you refuse to see things for yourself.' "

I paused, took a drink and hoped I'd memorized it correctly, then continued,

"The Master added, 'You harm me too because you refuse to see me as I am.' "

I sat back and watched her.

"That's it?"

"Yes. I dunno if you've heard of Anthony de Mello. He brought a book out with a collection of these little passages of wisdom."

"And you memorized them, right?"

"How did you know?"

"It figures. Mr de Mello, he didn't also write scripts for *The Waltons*, by any chance?"

I got the point and felt like a horse's ass.

She leaned over, took my reluctant hand and said,

"Don't be so righteous – you want to sulk, don't you? I'm only winding you up. Tell me another."

"You've got to be kidding."

"Please."

So I did.

"A snake had bitten so many people that few ventured out. The Master was credited with taming the snake. As a result, the people took to throwing stones and dragging it by its tail. The snake complained to the Master, who said,

" 'You've stopped frightening people, that's bad.'

"A very pissed off snake replied,

" 'You told me to practise non-violence.'

" 'No. I told you to stop hurting – not to stop hissing.' "

I liked to hiss myself, felt it had a particular relevance for her.

She was quiet and I had to ask,

"So?"

"Deep … or is it a sack full of shit?"

I gave a disgusted sigh.

"And your snake, Mikey, the one in yer pants, is he hissing?"

All of a sudden, I was tired of her. I stood up, said,

"You're a thick bitch, goodnight."

Her face crumbled. An awesome thing to witness. When a ferocious spirit folds. Tears in her eyes, desolation writ large.

"Don't leave me."

SHE HAD AN APARTMENT OFF REGENT STREET. This convinced me she was some kind of high-calibre hooker. Accommodation in this area of London is beyond expensive, it's a realm of rarefied wealth bordering on lunacy.

Only drug dealers could afford to live here. Part of me wanted her to be such a prize tart. Not only would I get laid, but professionally so. Also, I could categorize her and cut her down to size. If you'll excuse the pun, the Freudian slip, was a hooker going to give me mouth?

As befits worth, the entrance to her home was discreet. No frills, nothing to tempt the burglars. We went up to the third floor. The elevator was as spacious as Earls Court. With a huge mirror. No doubt to reflect your assets. You came down in the morning, your reflection said,

"Morning ya rich fuck ..."

Laura said nothing, hadn't said much since the pub.The elevator gave a soft "ping" and the doors opened. She clutched my arm, whispered,

"If you ever … ever call me a bitch again, I'll cut yer balls off."

Point taken.

It took five minutes to negotiate the locks on the doors. Finally, Nirvana. We walked into a large room, heavy old furniture and a carpet to our ankles. Subdued lighting emphasized the paintings on the walls.

"Klee," she said, "and Jackson Pollock."

"Cash," I thought.

A figure rose from the sofa and put the heart sideways in me.

"Hi, Harry," she said. "This is my new friend, Michael."

He extended a hand, said,

"Greetings, friend, in newness."

His voice was reminiscent of Richard Burton and he knew it. His hand felt like a dead fish and the impulse to recoil was strong. He was of average height and about sixty-five years of age. Almost bald, he had heavy, combed eyebrows. No one has black eyes, but he came close. A snub nose over a loose flaccid mouth and five even, white teeth. He was dressed in black, wearing what I think they call a safari suit. Stewart Granger and Roger Moore gave the kiss of death to them, but the news hadn't reached Harry. He smiled and said,

"You're thinking I sound like Dicky Burton."

"No."

Laura poured drinks and said,

"Harry's the financial genius, otherwise I'd be standing in Peckham sniffin' glue."

Harry gave a mock gesture of dismissal, asked,

"And, new friend, are you engaged in the daily grind?"

"Excuse me?"

"Do you toil?"

"I'm an accountant."

"Capital – if you'll forgive the term. Perhaps we'll labour in wisdom, pool the perspiration of our financial brows."

"Who knows."

He drained his glass, said,

"Alas, I must flee. A maiden awaits. Despite my mature years, she requires ... my demands ... a spot of rogering. Till we meet again, I bid you kindly folk adieu."

I thought he was a fag or a pimp, and I was delighted to see him leave.

Laura sank into the chair, asked,

"How do you like Harry?"

"Gone."

"What's your assessment of him. Be blunt."

"He's a wanker."

"Very possibly, but he's also my DAD."

What I thought was,

"I'll finish my drink, leave quietly and not look at my reflection in the elevator."

Laura rose, approached me, and put her arm round me, whispered,

"Put your hands under my skirt. It's what you want."

I did and five minutes later, I was lying on the carpet, gasping for breath. It wasn't love-making. More combat. She had cried out, "Hurt me, please hurt me."

Now, she was curled in the foetal position and I reached over to stroke her hair. She gave a shudder and said,

"I'm going to tell mummy."

I'd done what I do best, I left. It didn't take an expert to figure out what the Laura trauma was. Out of her life too I could have gone. All she knew was my first name.

I left my phone number, neatly printed. Not that I thought I could be of help, I don't really know why, but I didn't want it over. Not that I was in love, but most certainly on heat.

Nothing happened for a few days, and I was back at work. The typists at the office were in rampant bloom. All short-skirted and an impossible age. Jailbait with attitude. Dip yer wick and extinguish yer life. Vanish over the horizon to boredom in Balham and raise young muggers.

No thanks.

"I'M TRYING TO STOP SMOKING. I definitely have got to give up cottaging. Life seems hardly worth living."

Brad was sounding hysterical. The limp was very pronounced and, could it be, he'd thrown in a lisp.

I asked,

"Cottaging ... some kind of real estate, dear?"

He gave me a look of utter contempt.

"Is that a joke or could it be you truly don't know?"

"I truly don't know."

"Time you read Joe Orton, boy. It's picking guys up in public toilets, having it off in the booth. Very anonymous, very exciting."

"Sounds very dangerous."

"But that's half the fun, sweetmeats! Add the spice of cops on excitement detail, it's almost unbearable."

"The police?"

"Oh, yeah, thing is ... they get to like it. Size nines take on a whole new significance. Is that a truncheon in your pants or are you just pleased to see me?"

I thought I'd join in the sub-humour and threw in what I thought was rather a clever one,

"Fair cop, eh."

He hated it and thus the joke endeth.

To divert, I told him of my last meeting with Laura and spared none of the details. He said,

"Aren't you the game dog? Rogered her, eh, you do surprise me. A disgrace to the profession of accountancy. That Harry sounds intriguing."

"Bad bastard, more like."

"Roll your own, wot. Surely you don't believe her."

"She'd hardly make it up."

"Oh, for crying out loud. She's totally off her trolley, a real friggin' basket case."

"That's pretty harsh."

"The truth is cruel, ask John Major."

"Anyway, I have an idea. See the bulb flashing above my head?"

"Let's hear it."

"If he is a child molester, then I'm the man to smoke him out."

"You?"

"Absolutely, set up a drinks evening ... I'll wear chiffon and an attitude. Invite the ogre – and the lady in question of course."

"What, you think he'll tell you?"

"Not directly, no – but I'll find out."

Thing was, I didn't know if I wanted verification. What I wanted was her and no complications. Plus, I didn't know how I should suggest bringing "randy dad".

It was taken out of my hands. He rang me.

Naturally, I taped him.

"AM I SPEAKING TO THE ACCOUNTANT?"

"Ahm ... yes."

"How peculiar, you sound shorter on the phone. Technology diminishes."

"Was there something?"

"Terribly remiss of me. This is Harold. Not Pinter, alas, at least not yet, it's early. Laura's pater. I wrangled your number from her. She seemed most reluctant."

"Just the way you like it, you pervert," is what I thought. What I said was,

"How can I help?"

"Lemme see ... mmm ... it's 8.30. Shall we say 1.30 for a bite of lunch? You know Rimaldi's in Russell Square?"

"No."

"Good Lord. Tell the doorman you're Harold Benton's guest. There's a good chap. Wear a tie."

That's it. I didn't much care for that imperative tone, but curiosity is the mildest of my defects. I went to work and watched the clock. I asked at work about the club, and I was told you needed truckloads of money to be a member. If a pedigree was necessary for White's or The Garrick, pure wealth got you into Rimaldi's.

The doorman was surly till I mentioned Harold Benton and wow, wot a transformation. He didn't hold my hand, but he came close. Leading me to a library where Harry was the sole occupant. A sherry decanter on a small table before him. He asked,

"Our man here ..."

He indicated the doorman without looking at him,

"He treat you right?"

I thought, "Fuck the surly bastard," and said,

"Not really."

"Oh, dear, we'll have to investigate that. I was quite clear in my instructions."

I didn't look at the doorman either as he was dismissed. Harry waved me to sit down. Another safari suit, powder blue this time. I shuddered as I visualized a wardrobe full of them, and instantly remembered the occasion I'd met Laura. She asked what my name was. Then she'd said,

"I think I'll call you Harry. You look like one ... you dirty Harry."

I couldn't believe I looked anything like this reptile. Christ, did I remind her of this evil fuck?

He poured the sherry, said,

"Chin chin."

It tasted sweet. When he asked how it was, I told him that.

He began to massage his bald dome in an itchy sensuous manner. His eyes locked on mine and he asked,

"Are you familiar with Baudelaire?"

"Not really."

"What a pity, but perhaps we'll alter that. Baudelaire developed a loathing for physical relations. I mention this at the outset for you to note. In light of what might transpire."

His voice was in full Burton flow. Hard as it is to concede, it was commanding.

"Picture, if you will, how Baudelaire looked. A slim figure, always in black with a gold belt. Pink gloves, coloured cravats, dainty shoes. You smile, Michael. A touch of homophobia rising, perchance?"

I said it then. I can't friggin' believe I said the line I most despise,

"My best friend is gay."

And got my dues. He gave me a smile of amused contempt. His shining white teeth like a row of vindication. Then his voice raised.

"Is it possible to prolong a relationship with a creature who has no appreciation for one's efforts, who hinders them through malice or ignorance, and considers one as no more than her servant or property and with whom it's impossible to discuss politics or literature, in short, someone who closes her mind to anything I would teach her and who doesn't think anything of me, isn't interested in my work?"

He drained his sherry, then said,

"You think I speak of Laura?"

I did.

"In fact, it's a letter Baudelaire wrote to his man – all about Jeanne Duval. A lady – perhaps even lesbian – to whom he was attracted by almost pathological hatred. Indeed, one of the classic hatred affairs of all time. Let's talk about money. Do pour the sherry."

I did.

He said,

"Tell me."

"What?"

"About money. Its importance to and for you. How much of it you have but more relevant – how much you want. As opposed to need."

"Jeez, that's a lot of questions."

He waited, so I said,

"I don't know you, Harry. I don't know anyone well enough to talk to them about that."

"You will, Michael, you will."

"No offence, but I doubt it."

"Let's eat."

I looked at my watch, shrugged a regret I didn't feel, and said,

"Alas, I don't have time, my lunch is already over."

He stood as I did. Put his arm round my shoulder, said,

"Robertson said take all the time you need."

Robertson is my boss. I think I'd met him twice and fleetingly. Harry chuckled, a sound that had to be heard to be believed. Like unplugging a foul sink.

"Old Robertson's not the worst … stick in the mud, but plays off a nine handicap. He doesn't pay you enough."

I'd had my first lesson in serious money. What it buys is juice and I'd experienced it right up close.

The dining-room was not unlike the reading-room at the British Museum. Same air of seriousness and melancholy. Harry said,

"Might I recommend the trout?"

"Actually a pork chop would do nicely."

"I might have to insist on the trout."

The waiter stood discreetly to Harry's left. Harry looked to him. He said in a waiter's tone,

"Alas, the … ahm … ahm … chops are … off."

"What would you recommend, Jenkins?"

"Some rather lovely rainbow trout just in."

We had the fucking trout. Worse, it was delicious.

Harry ate his in fast furious bites, as if he feared it would escape. Finished, he said,

"Good?"

"Not bad."

"It's been suggested that Baudelaire had an unfulfilled desire for incest."

"A bit taken with him, aren't you?"

"Laura's an imaginative girl. She's had some problems and is given to – shall we say – flights of fancy. No doubt she gave you the impression I fucked her."

I physically choked and doubled over in a fit of coughing. Harry jumped up, grabbed me under the shoulders and began the Heimlich Maneuver. He was killing me.

"For fuckssake stop ... I'm alright ... just some water."

He clicked his fingers and I got the water. What I noticed was the speed with which he moved. As he settled, I said,

"Where's Laura?"

"Took off for Paris for a spot of shopping. Such an impatient filly ... can't apply the same expectations to thoroughbreds, eh, more rarefied atmosphere."

I concluded the fucker was nuts – wealthy with it, vicious with it, but stark raving bonkers. No question.

The thought came,

"Harry, you wouldn't be warning me off here. Is that what this is?"

"Au contraire, mon ami. I come with invitation. I'm having a little soirée this Sunday. It's my sixty-fifth birthday. Bring your gay friend. Sorry, your best friend. At the penthouse, say eightish."

"Will Laura be there?"

"Who knows, kemo sabe. But we shall be as jolly as we can manage. I did wish to discuss the prospect of you doing some work,

but I fear your cavalier attitude has scotched that. Do you resent my bluntness?"

"I'm not hurting, Harry."

"May I beg to disagree. We are all of us hurting. It's what we do with the hurt that distinguishes – or extinguishes. Must dash."

Which is literally how he left – dashing – in that friggin' blue safari suit. Like a bad Truman Capote. I sat wondering if I'd been stiffed with the bill. Very worrying when no prices are displayed. I felt even the fisherman would be on the percentage. I called Jenkins.

"Sir?"

"The bill ..."

"On Mr Benton's account."

"Oh, well have a hefty tip then."

"As Sir wishes."

The doorman was warmth personified.

"Might I call a cab for Sir?"

"You might fuck off."

There's all kinds of juice.

THE SQUEEZE BEGAN.

I was summoned to Robertson's office. A look from the typing pool – of expectancy. Either I was up or out. It made me briefly interesting.

He was on the phone as I entered, waved me to a chair. As I waited, I glanced around. Lots of framed golfing pictures. The inevitable Bob Hope tournament. Old Bob looking as if they'd plugged him in briefly. No one knew for sure if he'd died or not, but they kept him on ice for the annual event.

Robertson himself was tall, with a stockbroker's face. It revealed nothing, save he was in business – you were to believe serious business. Spare brown hair was heavily combed from the back to disguise the loss. It proclaimed,

"Rapidly balding man."

He had the suit necessary to his level. Bespoked, but not extravagant. You knew it was good without knowing how, or indeed why. His face had the ruddy colour of the weekend sailor. A bare desk except for the family portrait; it looked like a photofit.

He put down the phone.

"Young Shorts, eh."

"Shaw … Sir."

"Course it is. Are you a golfing man?""

"No, Sir."

"Better change that, Shaw – wot, get out on the links. Do you the power of good."

I didn't know how to reply so I didn't. He sat down and laced his fingers together.

"Mr Benton is considering bringing his accounts to us. Need I say what a considerable asset that would be. He speaks very highly of you."

"Thank you, Sir."

"You might be the pendulum that swings to our favour and finalizes his decision. So take all the time you need for his … wishes."

"Yes, Sir."

"We wouldn't want to lose this, Shaw … In fact, we daren't. Are you with me?"

"Completely."

"Good man. Give it your best swing – right up the fairway, land us that hole in one. I've my eye on you, don't disappoint me."

I was telling this to Brad who said,

"So you told him to go fuck himself … right?"

"In not as many words."

"How many?"

"Two."

"You said, 'thank you' – jeez, where's your ball, Mike?"

Next day, a letter arrived from the Inland Revenue. Some error had been made on the amount of death duties for my mother's estate. A new assessment would have to be made. I half-expected them to propose I take golf lessons. Harry had been busy. Leaving me poised on the edge of annihilation and success. Was I worried.

Badly.

On Saturday, Brenda came round. I resolved to tell her nothing – no matter how tempted. She had bought faded blue jeans and they just didn't fit her right. They sagged in all the wrong places, like age. It pierced my heart that she'd made the effort. Plus a white short shirt with the logo,

"I'm a Gas."

Jesus.

A pair of pink Reeboks that screamed, "new". It was like seeing Barbara Cartland in a tracksuit.

"How do I look?"

"Wow, Brenda, it really works."

"I want us to work, Michael, so you won't leave me."

Fuck on a moped.

Then I told her everything. Did I leave anything out?

No.

"Did you make love to her, Michael?"

"Yes, yes I did."

"But you were drunk, weren't you?"

"Ahm … yes."

"I'll be able to forgive you."

The upshot was I asked her to Harry's party. I nearly asked her to marry me.

"You asked Brenda to the party? Are you out of your fuckin' tree?"

"Look, she was in bad shape. Christ, she was wearing jeans – and Reeboks."

"Oh, horrors, she was fucked. *Jeans* – no wonder the Tories are going under. Still, it might work, eh? Get old Harry off yer back."

"What do you know of Baudelaire?"

"*Les Fleurs du mal* is all I really know. He seems to have regarded women as evil and morally corrupting."

"I think Brenda might agree with him on that one, in light of recent events."

"He was tried for obscenity for that book. I don't think he ever recovered – why?"

"Harry's obsessed with him."

"And you're obsessed with Harry."

"You mean Laura."

"Quelle est la différence?"

"You'll come to the party."

"Wouldn't miss it for a night with Bob Redford."

Brad took off for class. In between assignments abroad he taught at a college on the King's Road. A stack of books were sitting on his table. I flicked through them, mostly by Adam Mars-Jones, most with the AIDS theme. Brad called it "the literature of defence".

"Know your enemy well lest it become you."

Brad was currently of the belief that the only safe sex was no sex.

"Thing is, then you get drunk, and it's any sex."

I'd said,

"But condoms are protective, right?"

"They burst."

Harry's birthday, should I bring a gift? Since it was for a guy with everything. Especially somebody who was squeezing the life outa me. No present would be the gutsy thing. But I didn't want to be embarrassed. Moral cowardice, you betcha. I spent the afternoon in the second-hand bookshops. You buy an old book, they think it costs. Or does everybody go to Oxfam?

I found Baudelaire's book on hallucinogens. In surprisingly good condition, it was tied by a rubber band to a collection of the Liverpool poets. The lot cost less than a quid.

The title,

Les Paradis Artificiels – Opium et Hashish.

As I travelled home by tube, I flicked through an editor's introduction. The book was regarded as autobiographical despite Baudelaire's denial.

"Hashish," he said, "gives power of imagination and takes away the ability to profit by it."

Like the Italian football squad, I thought.

I left the Liverpools on the train. Let the next passenger have evidence that the Northern Line really is hell.

PARTY TIME.

I wore my casual gear and it drew the look from Brenda. We remembered the time of the microwave. She was wearing one of those sheath dresses and had applied fake tan. Unless she'd been to Las Palmas overnight. Anyway, it worked, she looked gorgeous. This was some miracle.

Brad was wearing a kaftan, tie-dyed bell-bottoms and lemon glasses. I said,

"You've got to be kidding, it's not fancy dress."

"It's the sixties, man, they're back. John lives – I love you."

"For fuckssake."

Brad drove a Mini Cooper and like a lunatic. He was doing that now. "It's the juice, man, I've been reading about O.J. Simpson."

"That's a reason to murder us?"

"Good as any."

He then launched into a discussion as to whether Harry was a child molester. After, he said to Brenda,

"You're very quiet – what do you think?"

She didn't reply for ages. I'd nearly forgotten the question when she said,

"As a potential mother, I think he should be castrated."

That quietened me.

We stopped on a double yellow in Piccadilly while Brad jumped out. He returned with a bunch of red roses. Brenda blushed, said,

"Oh Brad."

"Sorry Bren, these are for the birthday boy. Get the reference, Michael?"

Brenda had wilted.

"I don't, no."

"*Les Fleurs du mal.*"

"Oh."

Harry flung open the door.

"WELCOME,"

and waved us in. He was dressed in black ... yeah, a safari suit. About twenty people in the room. For a moment, it looked like a scene from *Rosemary's Baby*. The crowd were a mixed bunch in age, dress and volume. A large piano centre stage with a black man in a white suit at the keys. Where had that been on my first visit? I visualized making love to Laura beneath it. I know my cinema's clichéd. Was it me or was it the tune

"The Girl from Ipanema", or some equally unspellable place.

Harry said to Brad,

"You are Michael's BEST friend."

It hung there. We got the inference.

And,

"Who is this vision of loveliness? … Charmed, my dear – you've brightened an old man's day."

Brad presented the flowers and Harry gave him an over-the-top hug, saying,

"Just the touch needed."

The lower end of the room was awash in flowers.

I handed him my gift. He peered at the cover, threw it open, said,

"My translation may be shaky, indeed, risqué, but onwards. HUSH PLEASE … I'm READING … PEOPLE … PRAY SILENCE."

He got it.

Later, I discovered that what he quoted wasn't in that book. As always, he had other agendas. I'd just given him the green light for the Baudelaire he'd already intended.

"'I'm killing myself without grief. I don't feel any of that disturbance of mind men call remorse – my debts have never been a source of anxiety to me. It's not hard to control matters like that …'"

He paused and gave me the direct look. Not a sound in the room. His party.

"'Rather I'm killing myself because I don't want to go on and because the fatigue of going to sleep and of waking up again is unbearable to me. I'm killing myself because I'm no use to others … and dangerous to myself. I'm also going through with it because I believe I'm immortal *and* I have hope.'"

He clicked his fingers and two young men appeared with trays of drink – champagne and whiskey. I had both and so did Brenda … and more. When she saw me looking she said,

"I'm dehydrated."

The waiters had the look of trainee Mormons or young assassins. It's hard to know the difference. They were quick, I'll give them that.

Brad seemed delighted, applauded loudly and spoke to Harry in French.

Harry replied,

"Mon coeur mis à nu … Baudelaire said the more a man develops his artistic propensities the less sexually motivated he becomes. Only the brute cultivates sex and copulation is the thrill of the masses."

I whispered to Brad,

"What the fuck are you playing at? … Jesus, you're flirting with him."

He winked at me.

"Part of the plan."

Then to Harry he said,

"To have sex is to aspire to possess another."

"Touché," yelled Harry.

Brenda drank on, a waiter in full attendance at her side. I thought it was time to cut the bullshit.

"Harry, I half expected Mr Robertson to be here."

"Good heavens forbid. No plebs today."

"And Laura."

He gave a huge smile.

"I thought you'd never ask, Michael. Cue the music – this is for you, chérie."

They dimmed the lights, one sole ceiling spot on the piano player as he began,

"Tell Laura I Love Her."

One of those death-love-dirges from the early sixties. There'd been a spate of them. The guy usually got killed on a motorbike, but boy he sure loved his lady. "Leader of the Pack" was perhaps the best known. This one was right up there in the schmaltz greats – the pianist gave it the Vegas treatment. It was too awful for words.

Brad said,

"I can dig it."

Harry approached Brenda, asked,

"Can you sing?"

"Yes."

"Then sing for me."

"Will you ask the pianist if he knows Giovanni Pergolesi's 'Quando Corpus Morietur'?"

"He better."

I turned on her.

"What is this, I didn't know you could sing."

"You never asked."

"What? It's hardly a thing one asks!"

"I asked you."

I cringed as I recalled laughing in her face. I'd once read the chemical effect even a drop of alcohol had on Scott Fitzgerald. He'd go deathly pale, tremor, and become instantly nasty. Brenda seemed the same type, though she'd had more than a drop. More like a few buckets. Floundering for a hold, I reverted further into sarcasm.

"Some bloody irony this."

She drank more champagne, replied,

"If you'd read Tremain, you'd know irony is just another word for bad timing. But, of course, you don't read women, in any sense."

I was losing it.

"What, you're a psychiatrist, too?"

Her eyes were staring straight ahead and she said in a bland voice,

"C.J. Jung said,

" 'The meeting of two personalities is like the contact of two chemical substances. If there is any reaction, both are transformed.' "

Then she looked at me.

"Jung obviously didn't figure you in the equation,"

and she walked to the piano.

She sang like a person bewitched and God, she looked radiant. I sneaked a glance at the listeners. The men had lust in their eyes. The women just envy ... or some of them did.

Huge applause when she finished.

I turned away. Brad was waving a champagne bottle. I said,

"Get us a whiskey – a large one."

He did.

A man joined us, said directly to Brad,

"Look, Edmund White summarized gay history."

He turned to me,

"Am I right?"

"I've no idea."

"Ah ... you're straight ... I see. Well here it is.

"'To have been oppressed in the 1950s,

freed in the 1960s.

exalted in the 1970s,

and wiped out in the 1980s.'"

I said,

"What about the nineties?"

"Don't be condescending to me, you whippersnapper. You might be a few years younger, but I'll give you a sound thrashing ... eh ... Mark my words."

Brad led him away. He was still shouting and looking over his shoulder at me. I found an armchair and thought,

"If I close my eyes, maybe this friggin' nightmare will end."

And I slept. I dunno how long.

Coming to with a start, I looked around. The pianist was gone. People were standing in small groups. My mouth felt vile, and I staggered up to search for the bathroom. A long corridor led off

from the main room. The first door I tried was locked. A voice roared,

"Use the other room, end of the corridor."

"So sorry," I said, and moved away. It sounded a lot like the angry fella. Jeez, I didn't want to run into him again. Found the end door and tried the knob.

Harry was on his back, moaning. Brenda was pumping up and down on him. Both were naked. I closed the door quietly and thought I'd pass out. Then I did my best to compose myself and walked rapidly back to the main room. No one spoke to me and I left without seeing Brad. I tried not to see myself in the mirror of the elevator, but I did catch a fleeting glance.

A total madman stared back.

NEXT MORNING, BEFORE WORK, I RANG BRAD.

"Fuck," he said. "What time is it?"

"Seven."

"Call me when it's midnight."

"Brad, don't hang up."

"What … oh … OK."

"Get home alright?"

"Yeah, I think so. WHERE DID YOU GET TO?"

"You had a good time, then?"

"I dunno … too early to tell. Fuck, I'll tell you one thing, that Harry's dynamite in the sack. For an old guy, he's one hell of a ramrod … I'll probably never walk again."

"You … you slept with Harry?"

"Hey, Michael, how come you didn't tell me he was gay? Not that I'm complaining, mind, it added to the fun."

I was near speechless, but managed to ask,

"See Brenda before you left?"

"Didn't she leave with you? … Oh, right, she left with Laura."

I put the phone down. Was I going completely mad? I felt like I'd wandered into the script of *Cabaret.* Worst of all, I'd missed Laura. Put a call in to work to say I'd the flu.

I needed time to think or not to think. I threw back my head and screamed as loud as I was able.

I wanted to ring the Inland Revenue, maybe they could send one of their inspectors round to sleep with me. That might complete the circle. Whilst I was at it, I could ring Robertson, get him in on the act too. Bring his golf clubs and we could all get properly fucked.

Out of all the madness, the unknown and the rage, I did come to know one thing. I was going to kill him.

"You'd like to kill me," said Harry.

I couldn't believe it when I picked up the phone. I said,

"I can't believe you're calling me, Harry."

"But you're my friend, Michael, I like you."

"God forbid you should ever dislike me."

"From your lips to God's ear. Is it possible you can forgive my raging hormones – the last defiant shouts of an old warhorse? Everybody had a little too much alcohol, inhibitions got loosened, we're all ashamed."

"I'd like to see that, Harry, you feeling that."

"Don't be cruel, Michael, how can I make it up to you?"

"Get me a promotion at work."

"Excuse me?"

"You heard. Demonstrate your power."

"Ah, so finally we get to it, you do have ambition."

"I don't – I'd just like to see you jump."

I didn't know how I was going to kill him. But during his call, it came to me that I was going to need access to him. So I could bottle the bile, savour the prospect and plan.

If I could profit along the way, all the better. A plan began to take shape in my mind, but I'd need his co-operation. Some lines from an Iris DeMent song seemed appropriate,

"and with a cold one in my hand,
I'm going to bite down,
and swallow hard,
'cos I'm older now,
got no time to cry."

I didn't intend any elaborate plan. It had come to me simply and unbidden. I never even reached for it. Be nice to not get caught and the very basic outline looked like I'd get away. Tidy too, my nature wouldn't permit a messy scheme. Could I live with it? Well, I couldn't live with not doing it. That meant sinking back into the pit of madness that had embraced me. Now, the cold plain rage gave me lucidity and cohesion. Did I think his ghost would inhabit my dreams – probably. But as it was, the fucker had me full haunted now.

NO WORD FROM BRENDA. Yes, I was expecting a repentant one and I'd be outraged, hurt and mainly vicious. Difficult without her co-operation. She didn't answer her phone. For the first time I regretted a person not having an answerphone. I'd have left humdingers of messages.

Finally I could wait no longer and I called a cab. She lived at The Oval in a high-rise overlooking the cricket ground and she hated the game. The front door was operated on an intercom system, that is until someone removed the whole lock-set with a blow torch. Knowing the kids in the area, it was par for it. The adults use flame throwers. She lived on the twelfth floor and the lift was working. A somewhat marked contrast to the mirrored one in Regent Street.

This one smelt of urine, hash and curry. The walls were decorated with various suggestions, the gist being "Go fuck yourself." Some of the proposals seemed anatomically impossible, but who knows. I read until the twelfth. The door opened on two black guys. Wearing backwards baseball caps and L.A. Rams sweatshirts, they produced the instant reaction. PANIC. The white nightmare, you just knew they weren't Mormons. One asked, "Dis lift just come up?"

"That's correct, yes."

Jeez. How I wished I didn't sound so proper, so awfully English. Just once to answer,

"What's it to you, asshole?"

Dream on.

The other asked,

"It going down again?"

"I presume so."

They looked at each other and ambled back down the corridor.

Cautiously, I stepped out and moved to Brenda's door. What did I expect? Anything was possible. To find her in bed with Laura, with Harry, even friggin' Robertson. I had a key. We'd reached that stage in our relationship. Or she had as I'd conveniently neglected to give her mine. At the last second, I flunked it and rang the bell and hoped she was out.

The door opened. She was dressed in a white kimono, butterflies decorating the front.

"I didn't know you wore kimonos."

"There's a lot about me you don't know."

"Can I come in?"

"If you want."

Her flat was small, comfortable and ... yeah, tidy. She sat on the sofa, pulled her knees up in front of her, rested her chin on them. I've always thought it the personification of discomfort. Plus it looks idiotic. But this wasn't the time to mention it. A bottle of gin and one glass stood on a nearby table. Impossible to say if she'd been at it.

I wasn't sure how to proceed. Her repentant stance wasn't evident, and my behaviour had counted on that. Too much.

She caught my examination of the gin, said,

"Mother's ruin."

"I daresay … So, how've you been?"

"How would you think?"

"Well, I'm sure I've absolutely no idea, not the foggiest."

Yeah, I was doing it, sounding like Hugh Grant gone horribly astray.

"But I get the impression, Michael, that you're quite clear about the questions you'd like to ask."

"Just concern for you, Brenda."

Jesus, I didn't give a toss, the lie sounded just that.

She said,

"That's a lie. However, I'm going to tell you I'm in love."

"Good grief."

"With Harold."

I'd been sitting in the armchair. More perched I guess. I was on my feet.

"HAROLD! Fuckin' Harold … are you completely dipshit? After he poked you, he dipped his wick in BRAD … Yeah, he bopped the both of you. Maybe BRAD loves him too …"

"Get out."

"I beg your pardon?"

"Now."

I opened the door. The two black guys were outside. "What," I thought, "every time a door opens, they'll be standing there?"

"What!" I screamed.

"Wot de trouble, mon?"

"Woman trouble."

The volume of my scream had backed them off.

"We thought maybe the D.H.S.S. mon … not a popular dude here."

I didn't answer. Jabbed a finger on the lift button.

"C'mon," I said.

"No work mon."

"What?"

"Yeah, mon, like it don't go up, it don't go down."

"You mean it's not operating."

"Dat wot we say mon ..."

Twelve flights of stairs is no joy, even when rage hurls you along. By six, you're knackered, at the bottom, you're too whacked to be angry. I'd forgotten to even glance at the cricket. What a pisser.

A day later I had a curt note from her.

Michael,
It is imperative you return my key. Please do so by post.
Brenda Smythe

I friggin' loved that she gave her surname. How many Brendas was it likely I knew and *had their key.*

But I sent it. I didn't stamp the envelope. Small and mean-minded undoubtedly.

I BEGAN TO MAP OUT MY PLAN. As I thought, The Oval tube station was packed at morning rush hour. Next, I consulted the cricket almanac to see when the West Indies were due. OK.

Lunchtimes I began spending in the library. Got to grips with Baudelaire. I bought a good French dictionary to help. Be nice to kill Harry in French. Keep it in the Common Market, a sort of Euro-kill. Odd times, the realization of my actions hit me. I'd read enough to know that unless you were a sociopath, you couldn't kill without consequence. Not getting caught didn't mean you got away. Something in you had to die to enable the act to be done. I was prepared to accept that.

How much shittier could I feel? Baudelaire had written that man selects his prey, then becomes anxious and impatient for the kill. In 1845 he'd tried to kill himself as his life had become intolerable. He'd driven a knife into himself. At any hour of the day I knew a similar knife was hovering over me. When I kept my purpose, the knife receded.

I decided to test Harry's power. See how far I could bend it. When your whole world goes belly-up, a certain freedom follows. With everything screwed, how concerned can you be? Sooner or later, Harry was going to wipe out my job. So let's have a little fun.

I arrived at work to find my desk swamped with a recent government project. A job everyone had ducked, it entailed the most tedious of all accountancy duties – checking. I called a secretary.

"Get a box and sweep all this shit outa my sight."

She looked suitably stunned and alarmed.

"But Mr Collins instructed me to pile ... sorry, *place* it on your desk."

"Did I ask you about Collins, did you in fact hear me mention his name?"

"No, Mr Shaw, no Sir."

"Good girl, now we're trucking, we're communicating. Why are you standing there gawking?"

"Mr Collins won't like it."

"There you go again with that guy. Let me be blunt, I don't give a tuppenny-toss what he likes. JUST GET THIS CRAP OFF MY DESK."

She giggled as I stood up.

"I'll be in the canteen, have it done quickly and I'll bring you back a Club Milk."

It's heady business issuing orders. I felt drunk. A middle-aged woman with a hairnet was behind the canteen counter. She asked,

"Are you new?"

"I do believe so, the old order changeth."

"Is it eleven already?"

The official coffee hour.

"What do you recommend?"

"You're a cocky devil, you'll go far. The Danish is very tasty."

"Let's have that then, and black coffee."

"No cream?"

"No, sugar." Her name was Molly.

She was delighted. I nearly forgot the Club Milk.

When I returned, the desk was clear. The secretary looked anxious, said,

"Mr Collins is waiting for you in Mr Robertson's office."

"Do you know The Eagles' 'Take It to the Limit'?"

"Who?"

"Never mind."

I looked at my watch, gave a sigh, said,

"Tell them to chat among themselves. I'm due on the links. I think I've done enough for one day, don't you think?"

"They'll kill me."

"Here, your Club Milk. Eat that and then tell them, the chocolate will give you a rush. Today is ... let's see ... Tuesday. OK, I might swing by late Friday."

And I went. Madness is undervalued.

I SAID TO MYSELF,

"I'll just potter around in the garden."

I don't have a garden. But I liked the gist of it. At home, I threw off the suit and let it lie crumpled in a pile. I walked on it for effect. Part of me thought,

"Needs to be ironed anyway."

It's not easy to kick over all the traces in one go. But I was en route. Put on the faded jeans and said,

"My man."

The doorbell went.

There she was, finally. I said,

"Laura, I'd begun to think you were a rumour. You're almost a disappointment in the flesh."

She wasn't of course, a disappointment. Looked radiant. Dressed in a navy-blue tracksuit, she looked ripe.

"You look like you've climaxed. Might I come in now?"

She saw the suit.

"Shedding, are we?"

"In a manner of speaking."

She faced me, asked,

"Why is it you always talk like a wanker?"

"I'm working on it."

"Here's a tip, work harder. Got any sherry?"

"Sherry?"

"Is there an echo here?"

I got the sherry. I had the proper glasses, but felt further abuse could only follow. So I produced two tea cups. Alas, they weren't cracked, but I felt they gave a raw edge. Poured.

She took hers, asked,

"Haven't you got any proper glasses?"

"No."

Then,

"Would you like to meet my mother?"

And I near spilt the drink.

To buy some time, I moved to put a record on. A horrible dose of sanity hovered and I found my new-earned lunacy recede. Real madness chases the bogus. I selected

Bach: *St Matthew's Passion*.

Arleen Auger: Soprano.

Aldo Baldwin: Tenor.

It's not the best recording, but it's the one I have. The tremendous compassion of this piece never fails to move me.

I felt strong enough to ask,

"What did you think of Brenda?"

"You don't want to know."

"Hey, she's nothing to me, I couldn't care less."

"Well, she's one ugly cunt."

As the music boomed, what before had unfailingly been uplifting now sounded dead. The crude words like vicious concrete in the room.

I muttered,

"Old Harry seemed to like her."

"Harry ... Harry would stick it in a hole in the ground, and with some of the places he's put it, he'd have been wiser to choose the ground."

I felt assaulted. My face actually bruised.

Weakly, I tried to rally.

"And you want me to meet more of ... the family?"

I inserted as much disbelief and venom as I could muster.

"You'd better meet her. She's the only person who truly knows him. And you're going to need that knowledge. He intends forming you in his likeness."

"Come on."

"If you're not careful, first he'll make you rich."

"Mmm ... I could live with that."

"No. No you could not. Do you know who died today?"

"I missed the news."

"It wasn't on the news."

"Ah."

"Marcel Mouloudji. He was seventy-one. A leading light of the existentialist movement.

"The man was everything:

actor,

composer,

novelist,

singer.

"The Left Bank will be in darkness tonight. Paris is a poorer place."

I thought,

"How much better are we faring in London's South-East?"

But I said,

"I'm sorry."

"Don't be such an English haw-haw. Why on earth would you be sorry? You never heard of him."

But I'd a feeling I was going to remember him.

I said,

"Well, wotcha say, let's visit yer mum."

Laura had a car, an Audi.

My concern must have shown.

"You think I can't handle it?"

"Well."

"I've had bigger machines under me."

"Undoubtedly."

We moved at a brisk solid speed to Holland Park. In silence. Pulling up at a large impressive house there, she said,

"You can call her Mandy."

"Short for Amanda?"

"Short for Mandrax. She used to gobble them in the liberal seventies ... or is that the other way round? Whatever, as the current jargon goes, they were her drug of choice."

I had no reply to this hysteria.

The house was three storied. Inside, similar dark furniture to the flat in Regent Street. Laura led me into the sitting-room.

A tall woman was standing before an open fire. If she was Harold's wife, she could be anything from fifty up, but she looked late seventies.

Steel-blue hair in a rigid perm. A face that was lined to the point of caricature. Strong, severe features and cold blue eyes. Locked on me. Very slim, she had a long black velvet dress on and appeared ready for the banquet, any banquet.

Laura said,

"This is Michael, *the* one."

"Indeed, and an accountant, you claim."

"Yes mother, he is."

"In cheap blue jeans, I rather doubt it."

"Jaysus," I thought, "another live act."

I advanced to greet her. She looked at my outstretched hand asked,

"What is this?"

"Bad fuck to you," I thought, and said,

"To say how pleased I am to meet you … Mandy."

"Mandy … How dare you … such impertinence, and a lady doesn't shake hands with the help."

I looked round for assistance, but Laura was gone. Probably to the Left Bank. Sweat rolled down my back. She said,

"And do speak up, I'm an elderly woman. Don't mumble, speak your truth clearly, fear no man."

I took a deep breath, roared,

"Go fuck yourself, you wicked bitch. I couldn't give a flying fuck if they call you Tarzan."

And she laughed.

"Bravo, that's the spirit. Pour us some drinks, young man … on the table near the window."

I poured two large whiskies. Blackbush. Jeez, when do you see that? She had moved to the sofa and patted the place beside her.

"Join me."

More than a trifle self-consciously I did, but kept a little distance.

She closed that, clunked my glass, said,

"Bottoms up,"

and drained hers.

So fuck it, I did the same. It hit the earlier sherry like an express train. She said,

"Ask me about him – about Harold."

"Ahm … righty-oh … Good Lord, well let's see … Is he so rich?"

"Do the words 'as Croesus' ring a bell?"

"Right, I see."

"Harold is the supreme manipulator. He has shares in betting offices, travel agencies, hamburger franchises, golf clubs, hotels, etc. Only he really knows. He is completely without conscience. In one sense or another he violates every single person he meets and usually makes a profit on them."

I felt this was a tad exaggerated.

"But if he is ... I mean ... being as ... loose as he is, isn't he afraid of disease, of a virus?"

"He is the virus."

I laughed. Blame the booze, but I was finding it a shade melodramatic.

"Michael – may I call you that? Good. Answer one simple question for me. Will you do that?"

"I'll try."

"Has he contaminated any of your friends? Is there a person he's met through you that he hasn't touched?"

"Well, there's only two."

"Did he ravage them?"

"Yes ... in a sense ... but –"

"He was abusing Laura for years and I did nothing."

"Why on earth not?"

"Because I was afraid. Haven't you ever performed in a cowardly fashion?"

Whoops. I wasn't sharing anything. I looked solemn, as if I'd never understand such behaviour.

"It might be in your best interest to foster some healthy fear, Michael."

Laura returned and said in a cheerful tone, "So, Mother, has he agreed to kill him?"

"Laura, be a darling and bring us the whiskey bottle."

As Laura turned to the drinks, Mandy put her hand between my legs and squeezed.

She said,

"He has the equipment, but I'm not sure he has the attitude."

We finished the bottle. At least I think we did. I do know Mandy's last remark finished the conversation.

"SOMETHING IN THE WAY SHE MOVES ..."
Brad was singing and I noticed the limp on display. Attention – and guilt time. He said, "The heterosexuals get all the best songs."

"I thought that was the DEVIL."

"My point exactly. Jeez, who've we got, Tom Robinson and The Village People?"

"What about Steve Harley and Cockney Rebel or *Sebastiane?*"

"Missed that one, I was in Russia. Saw the movie though."

"Derek Jarman?"

"Fuck knows. He's dead so doesn't matter."

"Lovely language for an English teacher."

Brad wasn't hearing me. A look of infinite sadness on his face. He said something I didn't hear, so I asked him, "What?"

He whispered,

"I'll never live like that again ... never."

Pre-Glasnost, Brad had travelled to Russia many times. Not as a teacher, but as a consultant in the creation of English language programmes. Whilst for a similar time spent in Saudi or Japan, the

English teaching rackets would have offered him mild riches, he opted for fascination.

And had fallen in love with a young Russian named Petrol.

He'd given Brad a plaque of Lenin. It showed the leader's head and upper body. Hammered in bronze against an oak back, it had sat impressively on Brad's desk. As the trips were of limited duration, the affair depended heavily on letters. Brad had fallen down on his part of the correspondence for a time. Returning to Russia, he found Petrol had disappeared.

According to him the loss drove him "clinically insane". I'd argued the toss. He then showed me a prose poem he'd written. As evidence of his madness. He said,

"Read this and experience an unbalanced mind in its purest form."

This is what he showed me:

LENIN
AND
YOUR
LETTER

Your letter
stood with him
as if protecting that little plaque
you'd found
in Estonia
of him
and by candlelight
his shoulders heaved
as
if your letter
reminded him, on your plaque
and on *my* desk
HE
the greatest Russian leader
had no knees

"Don't mind,"
I'd say,
"Come on, sunshine
you had your day
the world for you
was on their knees
don't look so dour
The Russian Revolution
your finest hour.
Don't whine to me
bear it up

but I've got to post this letter
I'm determined
like yourself
get shot of it
today"

but I forgot

and Lenin on his plaque just moved that crucial letter that crucial yard away.

So …
    deep breath
Really
    I forgot
till now

Among my left-wing periodicals
I found it dying
to think
I was so much younger then
I swear
I wrote that letter
crying

and turned on him

"No knees,"
I screamed,
"You've changed my life
you bastard
so long dead

your help has ruined my life.

"I didn't need you
then
and I don't need you
now
What made you so imperial
you could change my life?

"You what?
you say ... your politics
would help my life.

"You RED
I'm RED with rage
my God
did I need you

"You have no fuckin' knees
and
on my desk.
I'm the power here."
and
ungloriously threw him
across the room
till later
MARXIST
so much later
I searched for him
and couldn't find him
or your letter

By nihilism
swear
the gods of unbelief
I couldn't find it.

... long pause

"Come back,"
I screamed,
"I'm on my knees
for you
come back
I want beliefs
come back ..."

but with your letter
he slid away

"No knees
you fuck
you third-rate
Jewish hack"

So it's the reason why my letters
and my politics
seem to slip away
unnoticed least
by me.

I'd asked, "Were you whacking the old Smirnoff fairly hard?"

"No more than usual. What do you think? Was I crazy?"

"Barking."

BRAD LISTENED INTENTLY AS I LAID OUT THE EVENTS since the party. Then he reminded me of his time of madness and concluded, "You'll get through this, like me ... You may not get over it, but you'll get past it."

I was furious.

"What, you're giving me a plot of *Little House on the Prairie*? Is that it? What do you mean, I'll 'get past it'? I just told you that I'm going to deal with it."

"Get real, Michael ... you're going to what? Oh yeah ... kill Harry. You and the extras from *Macbeth*. It takes a little more than faded jeans to gain a new personality. Have another read of 'Lenin', then settle back into accountancy, or is it mediocrity? Whatever."

I wanted to hit him. He was striding up and down as he delivered this homily. No, let me amend that, he was limping up and down.

I said, "You condescending prick. You think yer non-conformist job – your sexuality – makes you some kind of outlaw. Do me a bleeding favour, it didn't take Harry more than two minutes to get you to drop yer kaftan. You're the male answer to a tramp."

And he laughed out loud. One of those throw-back-your-head Burt Lancaster jobs.

"Aw, Michael, you're pitiful."

I stood up and he said,

"Run ... run away. It's what you do."

I turned and, holding my right wrist with my left hand, gave a half leap. Ramming my elbow into his face, I heard his nose go crunch. I wasn't foolish enough to hit him with my fist. Impressive as it was in the movies, I know it's more likely to break the bones in your hand.

This little action I'd learned from the Italian World Cup squad. The continuous playbacks had allowed me ample time to study. The slight propulsion upwards not only gave it force, it added a certain grace.

He flew backwards, moaning, and I went after him. Kneeling on his chest, I said,

"Do I look like an accountant now?"

Then I caught him by the collar of his coat and dragged him to the door. Opening it, I bundled him out and said,

"Tell Harry the Russians are coming."

After I'd slammed the door, it dawned on me that I'd thrown Brad out of *his* apartment. Well you can't get all the details right the first time. When I ventured out, there was no sign of him. Maybe he had a class or something.

When I got home I was definitely elated. My first violent act and I got off on it. The power surge. You didn't have to be tough or even strong – just sneaky and vicious.

I broke open the Thunderbird I'd picked up at the off-licence. Good macho name and it lived up to its rap. When I'd done some significant damage to the drink, not to mention my system, I picked up the phone. It occurred to me I'd have to investigate old Nietzsche. Maybe the lunatic had been on to something. I toyed with the idea of reading *Beyond Good and Evil.*

Now I reckoned, "Fuck that for a game of soldiers, screw the guilt trip."

Harry answered ... in Spanish.

"Digame."

"Hola compadre."

"Miguel, bueno, ¿qué pasa?"

"I rang to tell you I had to inflict some serious hurt on Brad."

"Might I enquire why?"

"He made shocking – nay scandalous slurs on your character."

"On mine?"

"I'm afraid so – and they were of a despicable, sexual nature. He has been my friend since childhood but I had to take action. I hope this doesn't embarrass you, but you're like the father I never knew."

A near gasp from the receiver. I used it to chug some Thunderbird. If he could reply to this garbage without puking, we were in business.

I could hear him clearing his throat, he said, "I'm truly moved, Michael. You know I always wanted a son."

Jeez, I thought, if we kept this up, I'd be calling him Dad. But his curiosity kicked in,

"What kind of hurt did you inflict? Nothing too major I pray."

"I broke his nose, he really did insinuate some nauseous acts to you. Animals were mentioned."

"The insidious bastard."

"Exactly."

"And to think I was on the verge of financially marking his future."

Here was the opening and I went for the *coup de grâce*, said,

"As we are discussing material matters, all you need to know is that good or bad, everything can be sold: it's just a question of assiduity."

His reply came in a gush of warmth and amazement,

"You've been reading Baudelaire!"

"Not reading – STUDYING."

"I take that as the supreme accolade."

"I hoped you would."

"First thing in the morning, I'll light a fire under Robertson, see what's happened to your adjustment."

"Thank you."

"I have major plans for you, Michael."

"I am honoured, Sir," I threw in that Elvis Presley touch, nice demonstration of humility.

"Call me tomorrow, Michael."

"My privilege, Sir."

Put the phone down, drained the bottle ... burped and said, "Not so bright, Harry, eh? – You thick fuck."

I liked the mess the empty bottles made. The crumpled suit was still in its dead position and I walked on it again for good measure. If this was losing it, well,

"Way
To
Go."

I HAD BEEN WADING THROUGH the prose poems of Baudelaire. As I pondered on my call to Harry, the bulb lit over my head as it does in cartoons. Racing through *La Fanfarlo,* I found it quickly.

Yeah.

"Samuel Cramer, who often astonished the world, was rarely astonished himself. He seemed to want to put Diderot's maxim into his own life and reveal its truth.

INCREDULITY IS SOMETIMES THE VICE OF A FOOL.
AND CREDULITY THE FLAW OF AN INTELLIGENT MAN.

"The intelligent man sees far into the immensity of what is possible. The fool sees hardly anything apart from what is. This is perhaps what makes the one pusillanimous and the other rash."

What a pity I couldn't read the piece for Harry. But I'd have to forsake the temptation. No wonder he liked old Baudelaire so much. The more I read, I couldn't quite decide if Harry based his behaviour on the poet's writings or simply found the echo there. The echo in the darkness.

I could see Harry's face as he'd come upon those lines from "The Generous Gambler".

The cynicism was carved in his heart.

"Never will you form a desire without my helping you to achieve it. You will reign over your common fellow men, you will be provided with flattery, and even adoration; silver, gold, diamonds, and fairy-tale palaces will come to seek you out and beg you to accept them, without your having to make any effort to win them. You will change country as often as your fancy decrees. You will grow drunk on pleasure and never weary of it."

I had to be careful I didn't get too addicted to Baudelaire myself. Already, I was thinking about him far more than I'd figured.

"I'M GOING TO BUY A BABY."

I'd taken Laura for a drink to the Savoy. Yup, that place. Where surliness is disguised as knife-servility. They tip their forelock and you ... well, you're expected to tip the balance.

Notions above my station? I hadn't even started. I had the doorman call us a cab after. As we got in, I palmed him fifty pence. Now he'd have genuine reason to call us names.

Back at my place, I sat her down and went to the kitchen.

I peeled six potatoes. Then I plomped them in a pot of water. Added sea salt and turned on the gas. Two roundhouse steaks I took from the fridge and sprinkled pepper over them. Beat them lightly with a rolling pin.

Pulled out a Greek transformation I'd prepared earlier and nibbled on the feta as I cooked the meat. Chopped up red and green peppers, popped them in a bowl of tzatziki.

Took a bottle of Retsina from the fridge and brought it out to Laura.

"Work on that, the food's coming."

She watched without comment as I set the table and carried the food in. I wanted to say,

"Yo, baby, no crime to offer to help you know."

But I didn't want to blow the mood. My mood as it turned out. I lit a candle, broke open some serviettes and sat.

Raising my glass, I said,

"Bon appetit … eat girl … go to it. I'm famished."

I sliced into the meat and popped a wedge in my mouth … ah, soft as butter. I said, "Jeez, is that good or wot?"

She hadn't moved, her hands in her lap. The steak in idleness before her. She said,

"I think I'm going to puke."

"What?"

"I'm vegetarian, how can you be so … so … carnivorous?"

I got slowly to my feet, said, "How can you be so pig fuckin' ignorant, but hey – no problem …"

I galloped into the kitchen and got a bin-liner. Back to the table and in one full sweep, I cleared the whole table,

candle,
wine,
glasses,
food,

into the bag.

The crash of glass and cutlery had the effect of snapping her head round.

But instead of an apology, she said the line about the baby. I roared,

"BUY A BABY? What is this – some sick friggin' joke?"

"I have the contract and money's no object."

"You can't be serious."

"It's already in motion. We won't even have to go to Romania. For an extra ten, the baby's being brought here."

"For pity's sake, Laura, hold the goddam phones ... Back up a bit, I must have missed something here apart from my dinner. Did I hear you say, '*We* won't have to go to Romania'? ... Who the fuck's *we*?"

"Oh, Michael, I want you to be the daddy."

WASTED
IN
WATERLOO

and smooth as silk
the tai-wan type, all flash,
if little durance
I supped on whiskies,
loaded there
till later
crawlin' on my bed
I slow chugged
on Thunderbird
and under scattered socks
the crumpled suit
chased a sweaty aspirin
to the wall

amid the debris
your confusing news
        cast off

I fell off
the nightmared bed
this evening
heavied Waterloo
near closing time
behind a gin or ten
I'll dare again
the story
the story of my father
lightly
        relate.

Before I could respond fully to fatherhood, there was a hammering on the door. Muttering, "This better be flaming good," I threw it open, shouting,

"What's all the bloody hammering?"

Two men in off-white raincoats. I knew *they* weren't Mormons, had the London weariness stamped on their faces.

One flopped an ID card.

"I'm Detective Sergeant Bolton, this is Sergeant Foley. Are you ..."

He looked at a piece of paper.

"Michael Shaw?"

I threw up my hands, said, "Fair cop, I didn't pay the licence."

"Might we step in a moment, Sir?"

They looked at Laura, chanted,

"Ma'am."

"We are arresting you ..."

He looked at the flamin' paper again,

"... Michael Shaw, for grevious bodily harm to a Bradley Howe, and must ask you to accompany us to the station, Sir."

Laura strode forward.

"How dare you come charging in here with your truncheons and big boots? This is not South Africa ... not yet. Show me that warrant."

"Who are you, Miss?"

"Don't you 'Miss' me, you fascist bastard."

"There's no need for language, Miss."

I said, "Whoa ... OK, I'll come quietly. You've got me bang to rights."

Laura shouted, "I'm Harry Benton's daughter ... that's Mr Benton to you P.C. Plod, and Michael is the father of my child."

As they led me out, she continued,

"Don't worry, Michael, Daddy's brief will have you out in no

time, and he'll have their jobs, see if he doesn't."

The cops let out a long, "Phew," and said,

"Who's fuckin' Harry wots-'is-face?"

I said,

"He's bad news, is what he is."

"Where's the child?"

"In Romania."

"Bit of a holiday, is it?"

"Bit of a shambles," I said.

They took me to Carter Street nick where I was formally charged. I was glad I'd changed back into the faded jeans. At least I was dressed for internment. Then I was put in a holding cell. I sat on the bunk and wished I had a pencil; I'd have marked the days off on the wall. As it was, I began to think about my dad.

I never told anyone about him. By vague hints, people deduced he was bad news. He was the gentlest man I ever knew. A second-rate accountant, he worked without promotion till he was fifty. My mother nagged him ferociously. What I remember most is he had ten suits. All identical and the object of my mother's wrath and scorn. He treated me always with kindness and generosity. When I was nine, he lost his job due to drink, and my mother ordered him out. I knew he drank but he was a better person drunk than most people are sober.

He took his ten suits and went to live under Waterloo Station. In the tunnels there, he'd put on a fresh suit, and when it was dirty, he threw it away. When he reached his last suit, he stepped under the 9.05 from Southampton. The express train.

I'd hated him 'cos my mother did. Then when I understood who she was, I began to comprehend him. I took up accountancy as a means of getting close to him. I read once that Hemingway's mother sent him the gun that his father used to kill himself. My mother would never have gone in for such studied viciousness. But when she died and I had to clear out her things, I found a train timetable for the arrivals at Waterloo. Maybe she thought he'd finally found speed.

I was in the cell for four hours. In time for afternoon tea. At last I got my wish and had a cup with a crack. It was heavily sugared and an odd colour, but I drank it. I asked the cop,

"Got a cigarette?"

He didn't answer and I don't smoke, but I felt I should make some nod towards the movie clichés. Bolton came and opened the cell, stood in the doorway.

"Your brief is here. The charge has been dropped. I don't know how that was arranged as the complainant was adamant this morning. So you're free to go."

As I moved to go, he grabbed my arm.

"I'll be keeping an eye on you, Shaw. Something rotten here and I don't like it."

"Are you threatening me, Sergeant?"

"That's Detective Sergeant to you, sonny, and yes – yes, I am. Watch yer step."

"Thank you for the tea."

The brief had been provided of course, by Harry.

My hand.

I said,

"No doubt I'll see a great many changes, take me some time to adapt."

"Excuse me?"

"Nothing. How did Harry get the charges dropped?"

"I've no idea."

"Course you do, who'd know better?"

"He paid him."

"That will do it."

"It did."

At home, Laura was gone. To Mothercare, no doubt. Checked the fridge, the second bottle of Retsina still there. So I had some of that. Freedom tasted like more of the same. I'd learnt one thing–how much I regretted never saying goodbye to my father. I wanted to weep for his stupid suits, all ten of them.

IT WAS SIGNIFICANT TIMES. Kepler Wessels was leading out South Africa's first team to play a Test at Lord's since 1965. Denis Crompton, the legend, was on the news. He'd predicted a 2–1 victory for England. The South Africans had a four-man-team attack. Led by Allan Donald, he had 63 wickets in 14 Tests.

I wasn't so sure about Denis Crompton's prediction. Mike Atherton would have to find 20 wickets. The wrist spin of Ian Salisbury would be severely examined.

England had already conceded eight hundreds in 15 Tests. The bowlers couldn't be too keen on facing Gary Kirsten, who had scored a docile hundred *and* a single in his last three innings.

What concerned me most were the last two Tests. At Headingly and The Oval. Very near the time now. The ticket demand for this first Test at Lord's had been huge. Record crowds were expected. As long as they showed up at The Oval for the third one, I'd be on track.

"Well, you know what they say about the Pope. He has no card sense, but he loves to play."

Next morning I poached some eggs, made milk toast and brewed some strong tea. Laid it *all* out. Didn't know if I could actually eat it, but the idea was flexible. It was, I felt, what an ex-con would go for ... or was that a hooker?

The doorbell went.

Detective Sergeant Bolton, no less. But a solo act this time. Had the off-white raincoat though. I said,

"Bit early, isn't it?"

"Might I have a word?"

"Official, is it?"

"Not really, would you mind if I come in?"

"Would my minding endear me further to you? ... So come in."

He did.

He took a long look at the breakfast. I said,

"You probably sussed from the police manual the eggs are poached."

"You have an odd attitude for an accountant."

"Whereas you, Detective, *you* have exactly the right attitude for your work. The coat's a trademark, yeah?"

He took his coat off, sat down, said,

"Don't let me interrupt your breakfast. I, on the other hand, had to leave home without nourishment."

"Be my guest."

He did – and ate hearty. Drank two mugs of tea.

I watched.

Satisfied, he leant back, said,

"God, that was good. Hit many's the spot."

"Was there urgent business for this morning's raid?"

"Oh, right ... Well, I was a bit hard on you yesterday, lad. I didn't know the ... ahm ... circumstances."

"What circumstances?"

"That it was a homosexual attack, an abortive rape attempt."

Jeez, I couldn't help but laugh. He didn't and asked,

"You find this amusing?"

"Aw, come on, Bolton, who called you?"

"Mr Benton was gracious enough to break off from his hectic schedule to explain."

"*MISTER* – MISTER BENTON – yesterday he was Harry-who-the-fuck."

"Yes ...well ... as I said, I was mistaken. I hope the ordeal wasn't too traumatic."

"I think prison has made me a better person, more open, compassionate. I can hear the birds sing, appreciate the grass growing. I want to help people."

He got his coat.

"Very humorous, I'm sure, Mr Shaw. You'd be wise to know who your friends are."

"And you're my friend, Detective, is that it?"

As he got to the door, he extended his hand,

"No hard feelings, eh? Oh yes, I believe felicitations are in order."

"Oh the baby?"

"No, your nuptials. Mr Benton told me the happy news."

I ignored his hand, said,

"If I was any happier, I'd shit a gold mine. Sure you won't stay to lunch?"

What was the old adage, I wondered.

"Do it once
and it makes you
a philosopher."

I had no intention of going back to prison. I rang Harry.

"Mon père, merci beaucoup. Ça va?"

"Plus ça change, plus ça reste la même."

"I am so grateful for your help."

"De rien, we do the little we can."

"Might I take you to lunch?"

"Capital."

"There's an Italian place on The Strand, Benito's. They do a charming apéritif, would one be good?"

"But two's better, n'est-ce pas? A bientôt."

Well, I thought, whatever else, it was short. I decided to take the bus to town and left fairly sharpish. Just caught one of those automatic jobs before it pulled away. I breezed past the driver. He roared,

"Oi ... you."

"Yes?"

"Where's your fare?"

I'd forgotten my monthly pass. So conditioned was I to just flashing it that that I'd clean acted on automatic pilot. As I searched for change, I said,

"Terribly sorry, I forgot my pass."

"I don't know that, do I?"

I took a long look at him, said,

"How surprising. I got the distinct impression you knew every bloody thing."

As they say in the markets,

"Don't you just love 'em?"

I sat along the window. A fresh-faced teenager was opposite. He had a range of studs in his left ear and it looked painful. His hair was razor cut and his pink scalp looked angrily out. A long white T-shirt with the inevitable writing.

I settled down for a slow read.

If you love someone
  let them go
If they come back,
  it truly is love.

If they don't
  track the fucker down
and slaughter.

Made sense to me.

The kid watched me read. When I'd finished, I gave him the thumbs up. He rewarded me with a mega-smile from ear to ear so big it near ate him. Startling though, was the fact that he was toothless. Not a one.

I killed some time in Dillons, in the poetry section, of course. Flicked through a *Collected Yeats*, found "The Second Coming":

"He slouches towards Bethlehem."

I slouched on to the restaurant. Harry was there ... with Brenda. Bad enough, but they seemed to be dressed as twins. He had the inevitable safari suit, in black. What's the female equivalent? I guess a safari jacket with shorts. Also in black. Harry beamed.

"Miguel!"

Brenda didn't. I said to her,

"How are things in Kenya?"

"What?"

"I tell you guys, now I know what Lennon and Yoko would have become if Mark Chapman hadn't read *Catcher in the Rye*."

Even Harry looked lost. I sat down. But ever the gracious host, he spread his arms, offered,

"What will you have?"

"I'll have whatever you're wearing – whoops – I mean ... drinking. Yes, I think that's what I mean. For now."

They were drinking grappa. Fancy urine in other words. As I tasted it I said to the waiter,

"Whoa, hold the phones. I'm right off turpentine. Bring us a cold one, buddy."

"¿Qué, Señor?"

"A beer ... Heineken ... something lagerish."

Harry touched my arm,

"Are you alright?"

Brenda said,

"He's on drugs!"

"Are you, Michael? Had a little toke of something? I'm not criticizing – some of the finest minds this century have utilized narcotics."

The beer came. I drank from the bottle. Not so much rudeness as preference.

"Naw, Harry, I just got outa the joint. Still not over the ol' gang rape in the showers."

He sat back, exclaimed,

"You are on something, your eyes seem odd."

"No problems, Harry. My friend Detective Bolton's going to mind me."

For the first time, Harry lost the Burton command. Even Burton lost it. He sounded ... wot's the word ... prissy. Nothing less.

"Bolton's a good man."

I finished the beer, signalled for another, was ignored and said,

"And as Brad will tell you, a good man's hard to find. Jeez, he had to resort to attempted buggery. Can you get Luigi to bring me a beer?"

"His name is Antonio."

"Whatever, I don't want his company, just a drink. Hell, even Brad's hard to find."

The beer was slapped down beside me. I said,

"So kind. I don't think Luigi likes me."

Brenda said,

"Nobody likes you."

Harry sh …ush … ed her and then they had a little kiss n' touch. Loud and mortifying. Harry pulled back to order,

claws,
spaghetti,
garlic bread,
house wine.

The food came and we ate as if we were friends. Lots of grunts of satisfaction and pouring of wine. Brenda groped him frequently under the table. Half-pissed, I was going to grope somebody too. Just slide my hand under the table and touch whatever was going.

Harry ordered a flotilla of cappucino as he and Brenda lashed into a vat of pistachio ice-cream. He said,

"Eat, eat, dazzle the senses."

I answered in a quiet voice,

"What the paradox was to me
in the sphere of thought
perversity became to me
in the realms of passion."

He dropped his hands.

"Salut, Maestro. You are truly now a BAUDELARIAN."

"And you," I thought, "are a fuckin' vulgarian."

Then I took my shot, nicely aimed,

"It's not Baudelaire."

He blanched. Brenda stared at him.

"You must be mistaken, Michael. I'm never wrong, and never about him."

I took out a sheet of paper, written in Dillons, said,

" 'Fraid so, old chummy. Here, I knew you'd check as I knew you'd be wrong."

He snapped the paper, thrust it at Brenda. She read it, said,

"I'm sorry, darling … he's right."

He turned on her,

"Did I ask you for an opinion? Read the blasted thing. Can you do that much?"

"It says,

"'From *De Profundis*

Oscar Wilde.'"

The waiter came to check we were alright and got both barrels.

"What do you mean alright? If we weren't, you'd have bloody well heard before now. What's the time? … Bring the bill and make it snappy."

He paid with American Express Gold. It had been my invitation, but I wasn't going to war for it.

I said,

"Harry, I'd like to treat you to a special day. The Third Series at The Oval. I'll get the white boaters, the carry-cooler and we'll go by tube. Get the full flavour. Oh – and my treat of course."

"Brad said you were going to kill me."

"Well he would, wouldn't he? What do you say, is it a go?"

"Why not."

I GOT MARRIED ON A TUESDAY.

At the registry office in High Street, Kensington. If that was good enough for James Joyce, who was I to quibble? The baby hadn't arrived yet, but most of the money had been handed over. The guest list was short; we didn't invite anyone. Laura's mother and some Colonel friend of hers were the witnesses. When I was asked the vital question,

"Do you take this woman?"

I wanted to say,

"Why not?"

I wore my dead suit, the black one. I looked like a mild undertaker. Laura got right into the swing though. She wore a white number by Versace. The type of thing Elizabeth Hurley bursts out from. It brought to mind the word, "RAVAGE". She was exuberant. Near euphoric in her behaviour, she was calling Mandy "Mummy" and the Colonel "Hawkins". I got called a number of endearments, but I don't remember any warmth, any sincerity.

Mandy was dressed in a beige linen suit and a massive floral hat. The Colonel was in a three-piece suit and it stood like a uniform. You just knew it did as he commanded. Mandy called him Thomas. Laura had insisted we wear identical wedding rings.

"I want the world to know you're taken,"

she gasped. A voice breathless with Versace.

"Taken in," I nearly said.

No honeymoon as the child was due. At Heathrow and soon. I asked Laura where we were to live.

"Oh, darling, let's not fuss – I'm having the apartment decorated for the baby."

"Come to Clapham then."

And I remember her laugh.

"Don't be obnoxious, sweetheart. I'm a Bolton. Good heavens, I couldn't live in Clapham!"

"Laura, I hate to be the one to point this out, but it's bound to come up. You're getting married, you'll be a Shaw."

Horrified, that's how she looked.

"Oh, we don't need to be bourgeois, do we darling? I'd like to keep my name for professional reasons."

"But you don't do anything."

"Oh Michael, are you going to be difficult over trifles? I couldn't be called Shaw ... There's something common in the sound."

As we were being blunt, I thought I'd have a slice of the action.

"Are we going to sleep together, I mean ... Would a date be out of the question?"

"Michael ... Ahm, after a baby, some women need a time of adjustment."

"But the baby hasn't arrived yet, it's not even in the country for fuckssake."

"A little time, Michael, some consideration, perhaps. Is that too much to expect? Must you be so brutal?"

Well, the pay was good. We sat down with a coven of solicitors and I accepted a lump sum. Fairly decent of me I reckoned. When the figure was mentioned, I nearly passed out. What I most wanted to do with this bonanza was buy ten suits and let them fall under the Southampton Express. It sure got my bank manager's attention. He called me Michael. When that happens, you've arrived, OR, you're going to jail and sometimes both.

Harry was in Switzerland. Visiting his money. He'd had little to say about the wedding, but hadn't put up any obstacles. On the morning of our marriage, a man had come to my door with a small parcel.

"Is it ticking?"

"Excuse me?"

"Forget it, I thought you were human for a moment. My mistake."

Inside were the keys, deeds, tax, insurance for an Alfa Romeo. A single white sheet of expensive stationery that read,

FROM BAUDELAIRE'S JOURNALS AND NOTEBOOKS

> Love is a torture *or* a surgical operation.
> Imagine a man has lazy habits like daydreaming
> inactivity
> and is unable to make decisions.
>
> What if another man were to wake
> him one morning with the lashings of a whip?
> That he flayed him until he fled to work.
> Wouldn't you concede the man with the whip
> was a great blessing?

"Very cryptic," I said, "or do you just get off on the whip?"

Thus I drove to my wedding in a white Alfa Romeo. Yes, it

clashed with the black suit, but I did have a white handkerchief. I was tempted to wear a white carnation, but decided not to be flashy. No need for overstatement.

ON THE MONDAY, THE EVE OF MY WEDDING, I had gone to work. Sorry, let me amend that. I showed up. At eleven, and at five past. I went to the canteen. Molly was doing canteen things behind the counter. Her whole face lit up on seeing me, not a response I was familiar with.

She said,

"'Tis the saucy rascal himself."

"Are you Irish?"

"Most days."

"What do you recommend, something fancy, perchance, as I'm getting married tomorrow."

"I recommend you reconsider."

"There's a child involved."

"Ary, sure, what are you but a big child yerself? There's meringue here that's sinful, downright wicked."

"I'll have a slab of that then."

I handed her a £20 note.

"Oh cripes, I've no change."

"Get your hair done."

"I couldn't ... could I?"

"Be a devil."

She put it in her apron. I took a bite of the meringue and ... she was right.

She said,

"You know, there's few things more sickening than educated Englishmen."

"Thanks Molly."

"Ary, not you. I'd never think of you as educated."

This is what the Irish call a compliment. They flatter you mildly, but also lash your face. When I was finished, she came out from behind the counter. I said,

"You look naked without yer counter."

"Get away with you and give me a big hug."

I did.

She pressed something into my hand. It was a very worn silver medal of St Jude. The patron saint of hopeless causes.

Thanks, Molly. I heard somewhere a hug is a prayer in action. I felt I'd need one.

ROBERTSON SUMMONED ME. It was congratulations all the way. On both my wedding and promotion. He took out a bottle of sherry, two glasses, said,

"See those, Michael, might I call you that?"

"Of course, and you are?"

Bad moment for him, but he recovered and obviously decided to join the madness.

"Ahm ... Trevor, actually."

"OK Trev, you were on about the glasses."

"I'd prefer Trevor, I'm not one for abbreviations."

"The glasses?"

"Yes, now ... These are Galway Crystal. See how they catch the light?"

"But can they catch the sherry, eh, Trev?"

"I do tend to ramble on, it's an occupational hazard. Righty-ho, here you go. May I wish you and your betrothed every bounty. You're a young man on the way up."

I drained the sherry, looked at my watch, said,

"And in a hurry. Catch you later, Trev."

He was still muttering as I legged it. I never did get to see the light hit the crystal. There's a tremendous metaphor in there, but it escaped me.

Outside, I went,

"Phew!"

And had a moment of pure disorientation. I couldn't remember my grand plan or my next step. Decided to take five minutes and just sit. Off Villiers Street, there's a small park. Usually stalked by winos, it's worth the hassle. Finding a bench, I sat back and thought about that hairy few seconds. But willed myself up and resolute. I searched in my pocket for the sheet of quotes I'd copied down in Dillons. I hadn't been sure exactly what to slap Harry with, so I'd taken several. One by Samuel Beckett helped me,

"I must go on,
I can't go on,
... I'll go on."

A shabbily dressed black man sat down. I resisted the temptation to move. He was in his fifties and scrubbed clean. Hard to tell if he was from the legion of the homeless. London was now teeming with the Thatcher legacy. To such an extent that people were suffering from "compassion fatigue".

He began to roll a cigarette, so expertly that I wondered had he done time. Time to acquire the expertise. He offered it to me and I took it.

"Thank you."

"You're welcome," and he rapidly rolled another, stuck it in his mouth. A rummaging in his clothes to produce a box of kitchen matches. Lit us up. I didn't cough or choke. Faking that I smoked was just another step. He said,

"You're not a smoker."

"Ahm, no."

"Never no mind, I appreciate your acceptance as a token of brotherhood. Are you a shrewd man?"

Jeez, good question. Sly, certainly, but felt no need to say that. I said,

"I just got out of prison."

He gave me a calculated look.

"I'd never have considered that. To return to my question, would you like to hazard a guess as to my former occupation?"

"Mmm ... brain surgeon."

Of course, I didn't say that. He said,

"I was a peeler."

"I beg your pardon?"

"P ... E ... E ... L ... E ... R."

"Good Lord, is that some sort of reference to Robert Peel? The Bow Street Runners?"

"Dunno them fellahs. I used to peel down the posters in the Underground."

And the fuck I was supposed to reply?

"Well done."

"How fascinating."

"Ger ... off you never."

I gave the,

"Mmm," and he said,

"I never found me a woman, you?"

"Ahm ... yes, and a child ... en route."

"I heard on the radio once, that fella W.C. Fields – he say,

"'Women are like elephants to me.
I like to look at them
but I wouldn't want to own one.'"

I thought I'd sling in some folk wisdom too.

"They don't like to be owned."

Then he went silent and stared at the sky. I thought I'd demonstrated how liberal, compassionate and caring I was, time to fuck off. He said,

"Can I come live with you?"

"Ahm ... tad tricky at the moment."

"Never no mind. Probably wouldn't have worked out, you being a non-smoker. Do you snore?"

"Most definitely."

"There it is then. No offence, but it wouldn't pan out. Down the pike a bit, I'd have to sling yer white ass on the street."

I was on my feet, said,

"Really must dash. Parole officer to meet."

He stood and shook my hand, said,

"You ever start to smoke and get a handle on that snoring, you see Jacob, you hear ..."

"Rest assured, I'll remember."

I'd got to the Charing Cross tube when I heard,

"Yo, mistah."

Turned to find him running after me. Jesus.

"I clean forgot the important thing."

I sighed, reached for my wallet. His face fell, a look of terrible dignity.

"No, no, I don't want your hard won cash – money. When I was a little 'un, my mammie used to read me *Alice in Wonderland.* Mostly I forget, mostly I forget Mammie, but I remember this,"

" 'Would you tell me please, which way I ought to go from here?' said Alice.

" 'That depends a great deal on where you want to get to,' said the cat.

"It seemed real important I remember that for you, Michael, real important."

Then he turned and reached up towards St Martin-in-the-Fields.

I headed down into the Underground.

I WAS DOING PUSH-UPS, GETTING IN SHAPE, when the doorbell went. I thought,

"Is there anyone I'd like it to be?"

No.

But opened it anyway.

A tall elderly gentleman, holding a brown paper bag. I said,

"If it were America, you'd get trick or treat; as it's Clapham, I gave at the office."

"I'm Coleman."

"Did I hear you right? Coalman? All outa luck, mate, we're centrally heated, double glazed and grateful."

"Edward Coleman, Harry's boss. Might I step in?"

"Harry's got a boss? Now this I'd like to hear. Yeah, come in."

He had what they call a craggy face, as if many lines had used it. Dark blue eyes, full head of white hair. A stiffness in his walk indicated his age as being seventy, in that ballpark. He was wearing grey slacks, white open-neck shirt, navy wool cardigan. They looked pleased to have found him.

He eased himself into a chair. I offered a drink and he said tea would be good. I got that squared away, brought out the teapot, two cups. He touched a cup lightly with his index finger.

"You heated the cups, well done."

Then he opened his brown bag, offered it.

"They're Oreos."

"Excuse me?"

"Cookies, don't you read Stephen King?"

"Not unless it's obligatory."

We drank the tea, had some cookies, then he sat back, said,

"You've heard nowt of me."

"Not a whisper."

"Well then, if you knew South-East London as you should, you'd have heard of Eddie 'The Arm' Coleman."

"What, you play snooker?"

"That too, but the story was I kept the arm – of a competitor – in my fridge."

"Nice story."

"Those were rough days."

I stood up, said,

"No offence, but truly, I just couldn't stomach another pulled-myself-up-from-hell's-kitchen type epic. Sorry, but I'm not in the mood for an inspirational yarn."

"Good for you. All you need to know is, Harry answers to me."

"Why?"

"Come on son, you don't seriously believe a degenerate like him could have made it alone. But he's got charm, a useful commodity."

"Did he abuse Laura?"

"Are you familiar with F.M.S.? No, and who'd fault you. Everything's syndromed nowadays. It means False Memory Syndrome. A case in America now where an accused parent says a therapist planted the idea in his daughter's mind."

"So did he?"

"The point is, son, don't act on hysterical information."

"Mr Coleman, why are you here?"

"Because you're family and no one wants to see you do something rash. We like Harry, he's no prize and is inclined to run amuck, but ... he's who we've got."

"You think I'd harm Harry? I'm an accountant."

"A good one, I believe. I must be off. I'm glad we understand *our* positions."

I walked him to the door and just before he left he said,

"That ridiculous nickname they gave me ... Way off the mark. Still, Eddie 'The Eyes' Coleman's no better. Despite how little room they took up in the fridge."

Next morning both England and my plans lay wasted. The cricket team were defeated, staggering play by South Africa. But more horror, Mike Atherton, the captain, was accused of cheating.

He put a handful of dirt in his pocket, concealed it from the referee. But the TV picked it up on his hand in his pocket, fingers and thumb pressed together as though they were holding a few grains of something ... and *then* –

A careful rub on the leather.

> Golfers pray for a rub of the green,
> mad clerics for a rub of the relic
> ... but this.

The tabloids were howling for blood. Huge banner headlines of

CHEAT

My murder plan for Harry was fucked now … and I'd been so smug about it. I'd invited Harry to the Third Test. When we reached The Oval tube station, I was going to bundle him forward, ahead of the crowds, to the platform edge. As a train roared in I'd push him. Pure simplicity. By the time they got to him I'd have been long gone and alibi'd. Just a dreadful accident. As he plunged, I'd toyed with the idea of saying,

"Daddy goodbye."

In that way, to appease the shackle of my dad and rid Laura of hers.

But scrap all that now. The visit from Coleman had unnerved me, but this fiasco put paid to it. A whole new scheme would have to be devised. Harry would never attend a cricket game now. Not that I believed he could give a toss, but he'd wish it to appear so. In fact, he'd be ALL for cheating, but contemptuous of being caught. So certain had I been of my idea that I'd ordered a safari suit. I reckoned that the sight of me thus would have diverted Harry's attention for long enough. The abandonment of all this had one silver lining – I wouldn't have to wear the friggin' suit.

It was time to visit Mandy. See if my mother-in-law had any inspiration. I drove the Alfa Romeo. No doubt you could easily adapt to life in the fast lane. She answered the door herself.

"Michael, what a nice surprise. Are you alone?"

"I think so."

She led me into the sitting-room. Again, she was dressed in a long navy number and emanated style.

"Whiskey?"

"Smashin'."

"What a common expression."

"Well, I'm that alright."

"Yes, I know, but try not to be. It's so tiresome. How is the baby?"

"It's more a question of 'where is the baby'."

"Oh, is it a boy?"

"Amanda, all I know is, it's expensive."

"She'll lose interest you know."

"What?"

"Oh, yes, she'll adore the baby for a week, then find a new obsession."

"You can't be serious."

"Michael, she's already lost interest in you."

"Oh that's fuckin' marvellous, wot a family."

"But you tolerate the trappings, yes."

"What?"

"The Alfa Romeo, the promotion ... the fat bank balance. Why not walk away – leave the lot behind?"

I said nothing.

"Your silence is eloquent. I think we might move on to a topic of mutual interest – dear old Harold. Are you going to take care of him?"

"Oh, I love that, beautiful euphemism. Why can't you come right out and say it?"

"Are you going to kill him?"

"Jeez, I think you're serious."

"But Michael, are you?"

Perhaps the drink helped. But whatever reason, I laid out the whole story,

Harry's party,
my aborted plan,
my father.

When I'd finished she said,

"I think you'll have to carry that through."

"And Coleman?"

"I'll deal with him."

I stood up, not exactly sure if we'd settled something or not. As I stood on the doorstep, she said,

"My chief strength has been, I never give advice … or heed it."

She touched my cheek with the palm of her hand, added,

"Do it soon, very soon."

I arrived at Clapham with no plan. To add to that, I had a letter from Brad. It wasn't addressed, dated or re-*dear*-ed.

It read,

Michael,

I am writing to you to not forgive you. So scratch that for a game of soldiers. Au contraire. I shall warn you at the first opportunity. Be assured of that.

My ruined nose complements my gamey leg and both are your doing. Am I bitter? Very.

But I don't hate you, Michael, I loathe you. And you had the effrontery to call me a tramp. Who – dare I ask – has sold everything and everyone for money?

I am in regular touch with "Childe Harolde" and he is cognisant with your plan to murder him. When we had our "killing" conversation, I'd taken a leaf out of your book. Yes, sweetmeats, I taped you. Is that a kick or what?

Of course, you ask, do our childhood ties mean nothing? I'm not an ogre, I didn't give it to him. Relieved?

No, I wouldn't give it, Michael. I sold it to his solicitor. Try killing him now. It's rather delicious he's now yer father-in-law. You'd be better take tremendous care of him. I've been listening to the sound of your heart, does it beat a tad faster?

I'll finish with a few lines from Fred Exley's A Fan's Notes. *I think they were written for thee. May you rot in hell,*

Bradley

... it is always precisely at this moment that a quick and heavy blackness scuttles the dream (as fleeting as the shuttering of a lens this blackness is); and when again the vision comes, instead of walking on I find that I am running fatefully in their direction.

Next morning, I re-read Brad's letter. Nope, no matter how I interpreted it, I couldn't find any evidence that he loved me.

"Strike one," I said.

I got in the car and felt for Nixon, what the fuck possessed us to self-tape? Burning rubber, I drove fast down Kensington and made green lights all the way. Coming up to the roundabout at the Elephant and Castle I braked hard for that maximum right turn.

Nothing happened.

No brakes.

Sub-Hitchcockian plots whirled through my mind as the lights turned red. A battalion of traffic coming at me from the west. I swerved wildly and the car ploughed past the bus shelter and piled into the stone rise to the left of Tesco's. My forehead slammed into the steering wheel as the seat-belt held me like an obsession … and lost consciousness.

I opened my eyes, groaned and wanted to howl. I was in a bed, hospital, and mostly in confusion.

I turned my head. Amanda was popping a black grape in her mouth as she read a newspaper.

"Are those my grapes?"

"Michael, you caught me. I was just testing them to see if they're fresh."

"And are they … fresh?"

"I'd prefer seedless, like Harry. How are you feeling?"

"Maybe you could tell me."

"Your forehead is badly gashed, may scar – and your right arm is broken in three places. Some ribs gone and you've been out for two days."

"Jeez, did I miss anything?"

"In the world? Or with your car?"

"Did I?"

"Well, the Rolling Stones have a new record, which may account for your coma. No, you didn't hurt anyone. Really Michael, I think your hearing's off. I distinctly said, 'Deal with Harry,' not yourself."

"You think I did it on purpose? Someone tampered with the brakes."

"How absolutely cinéma noire. You lucky old thing."

"Yeah, I'm so fuckin' lucky I could weep."

"Before you woke, I was reading that Michael Rourke is also in the hospital, what serendipity. The same name, father fixation and failed suicides – you could be twins."

"What father fixation?"

"Listen to this. Michael was shattered when his father ran out. 'I was always looking for a father. I needed him so bad.' You should write to him."

"Oh yeah, and while I'm waiting for a reply I'll wear dirty black

T-shirts and chain-smoke Marlboros."

"Don't be patronizing, Michael, You haven't the wit for it. Shall I peel you a grape?"

"Where's Laura?"

Amanda jumped to her feet. Whatever else she was, a jumper she was not. Yet she managed it in a stately fashion. Grabbed me in a hug.

Now I howled.

"For crying out loud, I'm in agony."

"So sorry, but you're a daddy. The baby's arrived."

"Flew in, did it?"

"Not it, she. A little girl, three weeks old. A tiny beauty and flawless."

"So, where's Laura?"

"Oh, for goodness sake, Michael, you really are going to make me CROSS. She has to mind the baby."

"No nannies, no nurse?"

"Well ... a few."

"Quelle surprise."

The nurse came and shot me full of painkillers. As I lay there, I mouthed lines of Baudelaire.

> "The sky's too close; it's like a coffin lid
> screwed down on one brought
> face to face with pain
> a grey lowering horizon. Not a rift."

And not a clue as to who sabotaged my car. Everyone I knew had a damn good reason.

DETECTIVE SERGEANT BOLTON ARRIVED. No raincoat.

"Wot, no grapes?"

"It's not a social visit. You could be charged with R.E."

"Is that a Catholic thing?"

"Reckless endangerment. No joke, son. You could be facing five years."

"Aw, do us a favour, check the car, the brakes were done."

"And you're suggesting what?"

"That you piss off. I thought you were looking out for me."

"You're living very close to the edge, Mr Shaw, it's only a matter of time."

"For us all, Bolton. Fights at the Proms, cricket's gone to hell in a bucket, but at least Cliff Richard is still with us. Isn't he?"

"You'd be wise to play the game, Mr Shaw."

"But I don't know the flaming rules. The horror is, no one else does either."

When I was released from hospital, my arm was in a sling and my life in tatters. I stopped at the corner shop to get milk. Mr Patel said,

"You were mugged."

"Yeah."

And began to recite the list of London crime victims he personally knew.

"Whoa – hold the phones, perhaps another day, eh?"

Manoeuvring with one arm was tricky, but it helped my self-pity. I'd had a thorough wallow in it. I managed to get the front door open, and stepping inside, the milk carton fell and burst.

"Fuck," I said.

A figure came from my living-room. Coleman, in an identical outfit to his last visit. He said,

"No point in crying over spilled milk."

"How deep and original, you ought to copyright it. Thing like that gets out, everyone will use it. What the fuck are you doing in my house?"

He spread his hands out, palms extended. Asked,

"This is gratitude? I've stocked your fridge, picked your suit off the floor, changed the sheets, dusted and cleaned."

"You're kidding."

"OK, I didn't dust, I'm not so young anymore."

"How did you get in?"

"Your lock is a joke. Come, sit, I have coffee and Oreos."

I did, and we crunched the Oreos, sipped at the coffee. He said,

"I used to skipper, you know."

"Wot, Merchant Navy?"

"Are you sure you're a London boy? Skippering – living rough."

"Spare me."

"Indulge me this time. I began to be over-fond of my drink. Eventually, I descended to the White Lady. That's surg., surgical spirits – two bob a bottle. Cut out the middleman ... and most of my intestines, living in Rowton Houses. Provided for homeless men by Lord Rowton, bless 'im. Then the spike at Gordon Road, they gave you a bed, deloused you. The white boiler suits after delousement. Even that became acceptable. Then I was saved by Amanda ... so I owe her."

"Might make a mini-series."

"Back then we had the Brixton Girls."

"A forerunner to Bananarama, no doubt."

"Mainly Irish girls who'd go with a black man. It was ferociously condemned. Not like now, it seems nigh MANDATORY."

"You're telling me Mandy was a Brixton Girl? No way."

"You don't listen. I'm telling you Laura has that mentality, self-destruct; let me show you something."

He reached in his pocket, extracted a Stanley knife. Laid it on the plate next to the Oreos.

"I took that off my son. It's the weapon of choice these days. He's fourteen."

"All this tells me wot, Coleman?"

"You find all this trivial, or even as James Joyce said, quadrivial. I owe Amanda, she's asked me to extend my help."

"Find out what happened to my car?"

"Yesterday, I examined it. Took out the carburettor, checked the grease on the bearings. Bolton assisted me. He even dechoked the cylinder head. Dusted the value springs. We laid out the crank shaft, tuned the starter motor and looked at the rotor arm in the distributor. At one stage, Bolton even lifted the hot-rod exhaust."

"For fuckssake, Coleman, so you're a mechanic."

"No, I'm meticulous. It was the brake linings that were severed."

"I'm so surprised."

"Crude, but effective job. My guess is Brenda."

"Wot, you're joking!"

"Have I somehow given you the impression I'm a humorous man? I'm not, not ever."

"But Brenda, jeez – I just don't see it."

"Young man, there's so much you can't see. I told my wife about you. How a London lad can be so bloody thick."

"And wot had she to say for herself? Not that in truth I could give a flying fuck."

"She had nothing to say."

"A treasure, I should hang on to her, if I were you."

"Might be a tad difficult, she's been dead for ten years."

"You said –"

"That I talk to her. I do, every day. She's dead, but she's not gone, not for me. Never met another soul I could talk to that way."

As he said this, an expression of infinite sadness took over his face. Took it and moulded it into something sensitive and gentle. Then he caught himself and physically shook. The urban face returned.

"Mind you leave Brenda to me, hear?"

"Aye, aye, skipper."

"And the Oreos, well, hang on to 'em. But ol' sweetness never goes amiss, long as it don't become the central factor. Know what I mean?"

"Sure, you're talking about biscuits. I think you're crackers and to coin a phrase, 'You take the fuckin' biscuit.' Yeah, crystal clear."

I WAITED AN HOUR AFTER HIS DEPARTURE. I was going to see Brenda and considered bringing a weapon. What did I have? Kitchen knives and a broken arm. Rejected the knives and there was a vicious irony in this. Which, of course, I couldn't appreciate till later.

I walked down the Clapham Road and my forehead throbbed. The hospital had provided painkillers, which I'd left at home. If I remembered correctly, there was a chemist near The Oval. And open ...

It had one of those narrow doors you squeeze through with maximum irritation. A middle-aged woman was behind the counter. She glared and snapped,

"Help you?"

"Mmm ... lemme see, some painkillers."

"For yourself?"

"Yes."

"Have you got a prescription?"

"No, I have a bloody pain. Does that qualify?"

We traded insults for a bit and finally I got some extra-strength Anadin. I started to open them, asked,

"Could I trouble you for a glass of water?"

"This is not a public house."

"Really, it's yer hospitality that misled me, I'll recommend you."

I was standing outside dry-swallowing them when I spotted a familiar figure, heading for The Oval station. Brad ... and no limp. I took off after him. By the time I'd bought a ticket he'd already disappeared. I took the escalator steps two at a time and got to the platform as the rumble of a train sounded. The platform was crowded, but I spotted him, halfway down, on the edge of the crowd.

I got to him as the train came hurling in and reached out as the crowd surged. Pushed him hard and pulled back. The scream was short and high.

Book 2

I cancelled my plan to see Brenda. Was that a serious error in light of coming events? I dunno, I think what was already in motion couldn't have been stopped, but it's one more thing to ponder. What I did was hail a cab and have him take me to the hospital. I snuck in and joined a line of people sitting in the corridor.

Tried to get my emotional temperature. I was close to hyperventilating. A sense of total disbelief, yet a voice chanting,

you did it
you did it
you did it

My hands were steady, but had one strange sensation. The flat of my left hand I'd used on Brad felt tight, as if it were still pressed against him.

A nurse stopped, asked,

"Mr Shaw, good heavens, Mr Shaw. What are you doing still here?"

"Waiting to be discharged."

"But for goodness sake, you were supposed to leave at nine this morning."

"I was told to wait here."

"Oh my word, it's all the cuts, you know. Nobody knows what anybody's doing. Come on, come with me. I'll get this sorted right away. You poor lamb, sitting there all morning."

The paperwork was redone and now showed I'd been at the hospital until two in the afternoon. Instant alibi. As long as no one talked to Coleman, I was clear. As the original discharge papers were dumped, I was given tea and biscuits.

The nurse said,

"Sorry the biscuits are plain."

"No Oreos."

"Excuse me?"

"Nothing. Plain is fine, I don't like frills."

"Truly, Mr Shaw, you've been an absolute brick."

I stared at her, for one stunning moment I'd thought she said "prick". Not that I'd have disputed it, but she continued,

"Yes, you've been spiffing about this. We're deeply appreciative."

And, I thought, "Hopefully very definite about the time, this time."

I went to the nearest pub. Mainly I wanted a mirror. Does murder show in the face? I ordered a large Blackbush and gulped it fast, it hit me. Another ... and went to the toilet. Braced myself for the reflection. Perhaps the eyes were wider, but that could be the drink. I hoped it was. To be on the safe side, I'd skip mirrors for a bit. Back at the counter, I sipped the whiskey. It tasted wonderful, like a rich promise. The barman said,

"Sign of luck, you know."

"What? What is?"

"Scratching your left palm."

I nodded at the plaster on my right arm, said,

"Luckier than this one, eh?"

"What happened?"

"Cricket ball, in the last innings too."

"Wow, must have been some fast bowler."

"Not fast enough ... not really, not when it counted."

"Well, he got you."

"That's how it looks, doesn't it?"

I gave him my best smile and took off. A side bonus of my hospital alibi was a second set of painkillers. Popped a few now. They'd warned against mixing them with alcohol. I'd had about as much of warnings as I could stomach.

It took a few calls to locate Laura, but eventually I found she was at the flat in Regent Street. I took another cab there and was beginning to like this sensation of being driven.

Going up in the elevator, I kept my eyes away from the mirror. Laura was waiting in the corridor. She said,

"Get ready."

I reckoned I was as readied as ever I was likely to be, said,

"OK."

She grabbed my hand and pulled me into the flat. A large crib stood in the centre of the room with a woman in a nurse's uniform at the side.

"That's Anna, and this is Isola."

I looked in. A tiny baby peered back, then closed her eyes.

Laura said,

"She likes you, she wouldn't sleep till you arrived."

"Jeez, come on, Laura, I'm not a dropa blood to her. The postman would have done as well."

"Aw, Michael, there's no need to be defensive. I've been reading about how new fathers are a bit shy at first, but you'll bond."

"Run her name by me again, just so I know."

"I ... S ... O ... L ... A."

"Romanian, is it?"

"Stop it, Michael, stop it – I want you never to mention that place again. Isola was Oscar Wilde's sister. She died when she was ten."

The obvious question in my mind, "Why?" I mean Oscar Wilde's sister, for fuckssake. So I said,

"Why?"

"Why did she die?"

"No, the friggin' name, why that?"

"It's important she have a proper name."

"Bit obscure that."

I looked at the nurse who never changed expression. Laura said,

"Anna's English isn't great, but she's working on it, aren't you, Anna?"

"Yaw."

"Might I inquire about Anna's nationality if that's allowed?"

"Oh, Daddy found her, she's from Iceland."

"Fuckssake. What, he's Daddy now?"

Laura moved right up to me, put her hand across my mouth.

"Don't swear in front of the child – and yes, he's Daddy. We're going to be a proper family now."

What was there to say? I'd stumbled into some extended episode of *The Twilight Zone*. I muttered,

"Wild."

Laura gave me an irritated look, said,

"Please Michael, do stop scratching your hand. I don't want the baby to catch anything."

I had hoped for at least one moment of levity with Laura. A sign in the pub delighted me and I'd been keen to share it with her.

It read,

"Genesis

is good for you."

But no doubt it would have been bad for the baby.

Dream on.

When I got home I tried to read a newspaper but settled for the book reviews. A full page was devoted to a book about Gary Gilmore, written by his brother Mikal.

It seemed his father was the person he really wanted to murder. Gary told his uncle that if he could have escaped the consequences, his first murder would have been his father. Instead, he went on to kill two men who were complete strangers to him.

I put down the review. My heart was pounding. Hadn't Brad in fact become a complete stranger? As if on autopilot I rang Harry.

"Where have you been, did you hear that fool Bradley's gone and topped himself?"

"Oh no."

"Where were you?"

"I didn't get out of hospital till this afternoon. When did it happen?"

"This morning, at the bloody Oval of all places."

"Damned close to Brenda, eh? And he knew next to nothing about cricket. As this amply demonstrates."

"Might we meet?"

"Yes, yes, come to my club, we'll need a stiff one."

I put the phone down and could only hope he meant alcohol. A Freudian slip was too nasty to contemplate, even disloyal to Brad ... fuck 'im.

As I showered I thought,

"To err is human,
to forgive is divine,
to murder is to complete."

Said out loud,

"That'll do it."

THE DOORMAN WAVED ME THROUGH. Somebody was learning from the past. Harry was dressed in a pinstriped suit, white shirt, Old Etonian tie. A sure sign he'd never been. I wish, how I wish, I'd known I'd never talk to him again. The whole conversation might even have been … poignant. As it was, I said,

"No safari then?"

"A lot of things have changed."

A bottle of Jura on the table, two glasses. He poured. From the shake in his hand, I reckoned he'd had a few belts already.

He said,

"As Rimbaud put it,

" 'I've come to think of my mental derangement as sacred.' "

And he gave a bitter laugh, swallowed the whisky.

"Rimbaud! But what's happened to Baudelaire?"

He gave me a look of pure hatred. No masks with Harry now. I thought he was on the verge of physically attacking me. And I had what, an arm in plaster.

"Don't talk to me about the dipshit. He let me down … and

he's not the only one. I put my faith in the wrong people. Treachery abounds."

I drank. Nothing to say.

He began to fumble in his jacket, took out some sheets of paper, asked,

"Ever read Holderlin? ... Course not, you fuckin' ignoramus. Listen – listen, you accountant.

"'If a man looks in a mirror and finds his image there as though it were a painted likeness, then he recognizes himself. Man's image is possessed of eyes. King Oedipus has an eye too many.'"

I thought he'd had a whisky too many, but remained silent. Harry's voice was now to shouting level and people began to stare.

A club member "excused us" and whispered in his ear. I can't say Harry leapt to his feet as he was too drunk for that, but his face had the thought. Slowly he got up and said,

"I must adieu and we never got to mourn Bradley, but such is the nature of the beast. Let us say we knew him in the fullest sense."

"Well Harry, you surely did ..."

"Tut tut, jealousy ill becomes you. I'm planning on re-marriage."

"What?"

"A man needs stability."

This man needed a straitjacket and soon. Before I could ask who his intended was, he leant over and planted a kiss right on my mouth. A wet dribbled kiss, and I dunno is it only my frazzled recollection, but did I feel a touch of tongue? Like a shrivelled taste of wet horror. Pushed him away, he staggered ... near toppled, then righted himself. On my feet now, I wiped my mouth with the bandaged arm. Harry must have thought I was going to strike him and God, I sure wanted to. He shouted,

"Assault your elders, is it? Come on, you pup. I'm adept in the martial arts."

"Or the marital ones – you're pathetic, Harry."

He picked up his glass and drained it, said,

"I made you, you hear? You're nothing without me and you'll do my bidding. If I say kiss my arse, you'll ask 'which bit'?"

He leaned over. The blast of whisky was ferocious. He said,

"I took Brenda to see The Tokyo Shock Boys."

And he sat back. A luck of utter smugness now. I was lost, one of us had totally dropped the thread of the conversation. Had I overdone the painkillers or did I need more? Gulped some whisky, mumbled,

"Did she enjoy ... it ... them ... wotever?"

"You don't enjoy ... you appreciate. They're a comic quartet – they position firecrackers on their private parts, even ram fireworks up their rectums. One of them, Gyuzo, drinks bleach. But alas, for their London show they're somewhat restricted, damn fire laws and animal regulations in this country."

I said,

"Animal regulations?"

"Bloody cretins, I dunno what's happening to Britain. In Japan they close their show by putting live scorpions in their mouths."

My left palm was on fire, I scratched furiously. He noticed and asked,

"What's the matter, body lice is it? Keep away from my grandchild till you get it seen to."

My only hope of reining him in was to totally change direction.

I asked,

"You heard about my accident?"

"Drunk, were you?"

"Somebody sabotaged the car – what do you think of them potatoes?"

The man who'd delivered the message to him came rushing back. Put his arm round Harry and cried,

"Gentlemen please, let's not make a scene."

Harry pushed him off, saying,

"Unhand me, you varlet. Have you any idea who I am? You dare to lay your mediocre mitts on me! I'll have your liver; your children will be reduced to *Big Issue* vendors ..."

And he weaved his way out, shouting and spitting. I sank into the armchair; the man was wringing his hands muttering,

"Oh dear ... Dear oh dear, how unfortunate. Most upsetting ... so unlike him, he must have had a major breakdown."

My palm was a riot of itchiness and I said,

"It's that he hasn't long to live."

And I was right.

Outside, I hailed a taxi and gave curt directions. No doubt at all that I was sliding effortlessly into the contempt of money. Knew that I could be as rude as I wished 'cos I'd tip lavishly. When we got to Regent Street, he didn't exactly touch his cloth cap and say, "Ta very much Guvnor," but it was in the air. Pre-Laura days, I'd dreaded the whole fandango of tipping. Terrified I'd give too little and be chased by indignant waiters. Or horrors, over-tip and worry for weeks about extravagance. Brenda had been no help. She'd take out her pocket calculator and mortify me. Now I didn't give a monkeys. Tip like a bastard and relish their fuckin' gratitude. In the mirrored elevator, I peered close and had to concede I looked stone bloody mad, whispered,

"It's the painkillers, they're distorting my vision."

Anna, the nanny, opened the door, intoned,

"Madam is not in residence."

And definitely she was blocking my entrance. I said,

"I've started so I'll finish."

No response. I tried to explain.

"It's wot Magnus Magnusson says on TV – 'fraid it's the only Icelandic I know."

Still nothing.

"Hey Anna, lemme put this real simple: move out of my fuckin' way, OK?"

She did. As I strolled in I added,

"See, was that so difficult? You're getting the hang of it already. In no time you'll be bopping a Paki and collecting coupons in Hackney Wicks."

She put her finger to her lips, said,

"Shh ... quietness ... baby sleep."

I turned, put my face right in hers,

"Don't ever friggin' shish me lady, you'll be outa here so fast your bloody feet won't know yer arse from your Icelandic elbow."

We had our understanding. She fucked off to do nannied stuff in other rooms. I had a shifty through the videos, thought it would wind me down. At this rate I'd be burnt out by teatime. I shouted,

"Anna, oh Anna, if there's coffee going put my name down and a morsel to eat ... bacon sannie perhaps ... no mustard and no hurry, there's a good girl."

Couldn't settle on a film. Laura was fond of murder mysteries and I'd had too close a look at the real thing too recently. Took a concentrated look at *Slacker* by Richard Linklater. His first movie apparently. It documented a day in the life of a Texas neighbourhood. This area was populated primarily by dropouts. I said,

"Whoa-kay Rich, lets give it a twirl, see what you got."

I didn't get far. The rage pouring from the screen was too much for me. A band called Butthole Surfers had a drummer named Teresa. I wondered if they might be related to The Tokyo Shock Boys. Ol' Teresa was certainly enterprising if not to say downright crazy. She tried to sell a "smear test" she claimed belonged to Madonna. Switched off. Maybe on another day I'd be able for this but no way in hell was it this day. Jumping up, I shouted again,

"Yo, Anna ... baby! Hold the coffee hon, gotta jet – don't bother seeing me out, I'll find my own way."

A walk, I thought, get some of that London air. Largely influenced by the fact there wasn't a cab in sight. Ran by a gauntlet of street people, the like of whom I couldn't believe. None of your polite requests for a few coppers. Fuck no, this was all-out combat, demands with absolute menace. By Leicester Square I was shell-shocked and plunged into the Underground. Not much respite as buskers with every known instrument were on the make. A surge of manic intolerance took hold and I had to struggle not to push another person under the train. When I got home, I was knackered to the point of delirium but rooted out Baudelaire's prose poems. He had written about this.

Yeah, here it was – "Let's Beat Up the Poor".

"My man," I said and read on:

"As I was about to go into an inn a beggar held out his hand with one of those unforgettable glances which would overthrow thrones. Instantly I leapt on the beggar. With a single punch I closed one of his eyes, knocked out two of his teeth. Began to pound his head against a wall. Then, with a kick at his back, energetically enough to break his spine, I picked up a large tree branch and pounded him."

"Jesus," I said.

And sank into a chair, let the book slide to the floor. As sleep rushed to me I knew Harry would reconsider dumping Baudelaire if I showed him that. Yeah, time to reinstate the old reprobate.

Standing on the Underground I saw a hand come over the ledge, a bloodied hand, then another ... and start to pull up onto the platform. Bradley, a torn hideous form, groaning and bleeding ... and pulling himself along on his savaged body towards me, he was whispering,

"Mind the gap."

I couldn't move. A putrid smell was suffocating me and he grabbed my left hand, turned the palm to his mouth and said,

"Lemme kiss it all better."

Mother Teresa of Calcutta was reading from Baudelaire but at a staccato pace, and in the distance Harry was waving. My own scream woke me, I said,

"Oh sweet fuck."

And could barely move from stiffness. I'd slept in a curled position in the chair and every bone felt twisted. Rising slowly, the receding images of the dream gave me a final shiver. Tore at my clothes and climbed in the shower. With a bandaged arm, it was awkward to wash, but I let the water blast and pound me for near ten minutes. The phone rang.

"Is that you, Shaw?"

"Yes it is, at least I hope so."

"This is Collins ..."

"It's not Michael Collins, I trust?"

"From work, course it's understandable you'd be no longer familiar with us ... Might we expect to ever clap an eye on you again? There's dust on your desk."

I was tingling from the shower but in dire need of coffee. Best be brief.

"I'm concentrating on the Benton account as per Trev's instructions."

"Trev?"

"Robertson – our leader, refer all questions to him."

"Your days are numbered, Shaw."

"Ah, some accountancy humour – bit early for it, isn't it? Now clean up my desk Collins, pronto."

I hung up. A small, but as they wrote, Phyrric victory. It rang again within seconds. I'd dispense with innuendo, get some of that clear and direct communication ... snatched the phone, said,

"Fuck off, Collins."

"Michael ... Michael ... It's Brenda."

"Oh shit ... sorry."

"You answer all your calls like that?"

"Hey Brenda, was there something or did you just call for aggro?"

Her voice was odd, as if she was talking in a vacuum or had the phone at arm's length. Sorta throwing her voice at it.

"I need your help."

"You jest, surely ... I mean major league kidding, right?"

"Please Michael."

"What kind of help?"

"Will you come to the flat, now?"

Pay-off time at last, take the kicks when they're there.

"But Brenda, I don't have a key, you DEMANDED its return, remember? Remember doing that?"

"I'll be waiting at the door, can you hurry? Take a cab."

"You mean there's another way?"

The cab driver was that rarity, English, and said,

"Wotcher fink on the cricket then?"

"I'd hoped to make a killing."

He then began the cab requirement of a meaningless monologue. Tuned him out, though odd bits filtered through.

Paki bashing,
fast bowlers,
the *Sun*'s page three,
Guardian readers,
jellied eels.

Mainly I was wrestling with a dilemma, whether to ride Brenda or not. Most against this was going where Harry had been. To coin a phrase, I decided to play it as it laid.

As I waited for the elevator, I hoped I wouldn't run into the two black guys, but no sign of them. Brenda wasn't waiting at the door and I hammered with more than a tad of irk. Opened immediately, she was in a wedding dress. I instantly thought, "They're having the marriage here, now," … she took my hand and let me in.

Harry was lying on his back, his upper torso bare, black stockings and suspenders on the lower. His head was turned towards the balcony. I gasped,

"What the fuck?"

"He's dead."

"He's what?"

"Auto-eroticism – for the jaded palate – you are strangled to the very brink of death. It's a delicate balance to orgasm at the same time – bin-liners help – it can go dreadfully wrong."

"Obviously."

"It's the ultimate experience."

"Sort of come and go simultaneously – it was certainly Harry's ultimate one."

She was still holding my hand, said,

"Oh, that's not what killed him – look."

I edged closer … a butcher's knife was embedded in his throat. "Jesus!"

Brenda released my hand, asked,

"Tea, coffee?"

"What? Oh … right … no … I mean pour me a huge fucking drink."

She did and one for herself, clinked my glass, said,

"Good health."

I sank it fast, it burned but didn't help. I asked weakly,

"Did somebody break in? I mean … what the fuck's going on?"

"Harry had promised to marry me and I even got the dress … see, like it?"

"Very fetching."

"Well, I put it on to show him and he said he had a surprise for me – he was going to marry some Icelandic bitch."

"Anna!"

"What – you know her – you knew?"

"Good Lord no … truly … what …"

"God," I thought, "what new horror, maybe the old bastard's still alive."

Reluctantly I moved closer.

"No, Michael, you'll have to bend down."

My heart was pounding. I knelt but couldn't look at his head.

She grabbed my hand and said,

"Look at his face."

And she clasped the knife handle and pulled – Harry's head rolled and she slapped the knife into my right palm. Then she used both her hands to lock shut my grip.

"Now, Michael, we both did it."

"What? No bloody way."

"Yes, oh yes … Marry me, Michael, or I'll say you did it. Everyone knows you planned to. Harry's lawyer has you on tape. Remember Bradley recorded you saying so."

I jerked my hand free, rose and backed off up against the wall, the knife in my hand. I let it drop. She followed me.

"It's only my due Michael, I will be married … Do you know how much this dress COST?"

This she spat in my face.

"You have no choice."

The bandaged arm swung up and lashed her under the chin, she went over on her back.

"Go, go, go, go," I whimpered.

She was only dazed and I bent quickly to lift her, the pain electric in my arm. Lifting her was easy as she'd no weight, her hand tried to caress my face.

"Oh Michael."

Carried her out to the balcony and hoisted her on the rim. I looked into her face and she was smiling, said,

"Here comes the bride."

And let go.

Back inside, I cleaned the knife and bent again over Harry, tightened his fingers round it. Better of course if I'd Brenda's prints were on it but she was out. They'd hardly think he stabbed himself. Time was vital and I didn't have enough to plan better. Washed and dried my glass, put it in the cupboard.

A roaring in my head:

"Get
the
fuck
outa here ..."

Couldn't risk the elevator, so ran like a madman down twelve flights, again. The blood pounding in my ears was deafening. Outside, I had to force myself to walk and strolled to the Clapham Road. Now I could hear the sirens and maintained the casual pace. Didn't want to risk waiting for a cab so kept going. At Kensington I stopped and let out a huge "phew" and hailed a cab.

Ten minutes – or ten hours, I dunno – but I was knocking on Amanda's door. As soon as she opened, I bolted inside and made for the drinks cabinet. I had a gin bottle on my head as she came into the room.

"Whatever happened to hello?"

I gasped as gin ran down my front.

"I'm in deep shit."

She took the bottle from me and pushed me gently into a chair, fixed me a drink in a glass.

"Now Michael, tell me everything."

I ran the story by her. In my version it was as it happened save I claimed Brenda had committed suicide after confessing Harry's murder. She didn't look convinced.

"Mmm, Brenda told you, then took a flying leap, is that it? Couldn't you have stopped her? Not that I don't believe you, Michael, but others will ask."

"I … I was too stunned."

"Stunned! Yes, I can see how that might be feasible … stunned … mmm. You'll find your eyes a little heavy, I put a relaxer in your drink."

"What?"

"Just go with the flow. Amanda will take care of everything."

I felt the drink slide from my fingers as my head dropped to my chest.

I had recently flicked through Craig Raine's *History of the Home Movie.*

The narrative is interspersed with short verse. One of these dogged my sleep. A hanged man giving black looks as he dangles

"at the end of his tether
highly strung".

Blame the gin!

I came to in a large double bed, naked. Total disorientation till a body moved beside me ... Amanda.

Jumping up I roared,

"What the fuck!"

She stirred and sat up. God almighty she looked ancient, but at least she wasn't naked.

"Ah Michael, did you sleep well?"

"I dunno, did I?"

She gave a shy smile.

"Laura never told me of your energy."

"What?"

"Oh dear, the younger generation are so crude, no finesse … Well, if you must, your sexual prowess is admirable … What's the common slang – you're hung, big boy."

"And you're a friggin' lunatic. I don't believe this. What is it with you crowd? Banging day and night, anything or anybody, awake or asleep, drunk or sober. If it breathes, ye bop it. Couldn't ye get help, or sheep?"

She stretched, her nightie slipped down and she caught my hurried look – gave a titter and actually wagged her index finger.

"Oh, you're insatiable but alas, I must disappoint you … I'm not a morning person. One must allow some tiny concession to age."

I sat on the edge of the bed.

"Where's my clothes, I'm outa here."

"Not without catching up on … current activities."

"You've heard something, tell me."

"Tut, tut – all in good time. Your clothes are in the wardrobe. Now away to the room, I must dress … or would you like to watch?"

I went.

I dressed on the landing and could smell fresh coffee. Headed for that. A fully prepared breakfast table, like a hotel. A girl of about twenty was dressed in a maid's uniform, said,

"Buenos días, Señor."

I didn't answer. Sitting down, I couldn't see a coffee pot. The maid was hovering, I asked,

"¿Dónde está el café?"

"¿Café con leche?"

"Yeah."

When she brought it, she muttered something else I didn't catch.

To be on the safe side, I answered,

"Fuck off."

I was on my second toast when Amanda appeared. Wearing a long red dress and worse, a girlish red ribbon. What could I say but,

"Scarlet O'Hara."

Worse again, she took it as a compliment and curtsied. The maid whispered to her and a furious outpouring of Spanish followed. Then the maid fled to the kitchen. Amanda stood by a chair looking expectant. Then I got it, I was to seat her.

"Dream on, dotsy," I thought.

"Oh, very well," she snapped and sat. "You appear to have upset the maid ..."

"Where's she from, did I detect an Oirish accent?"

"Don't be facetious. Consuela is from El Salvador. Staff, suitable persons are most difficult to obtain. A Filipina had to be dismissed for insolence, a trait I will not tolerate."

The shouting blew out of nowhere and I ignored it.

"I'd like to have a Filipina."

Amanda crunched on some dry toast so I continued,

"Who's putting the pedal to the metal with ol' Consuelo?"

"I'm sure I've no idea what you mean. Aren't you curious as to your ... situation?"

"Well I'm fucked, right? Then ... now ... later. Thing is, is it fun? I dunno yet."

"Now, now, Michael, no need to be so pessimistic. Coleman was by last night and he sees no reason for concern if you've a suitable alibi."

I began to discern the pattern.

"And do I?"

"That very much depends, young man."

"On what?"

"Well, you're nominally now the head of the family. I see no reason why you shouldn't reside here."

"You're joking … and service you I suppose?"

"Only intermittently; I'm not a demanding woman."

So here it was, I was *capo del tutti capi* or some such shit. Mainly I was horrified.

"Why me, how did I get to be so lucky?"

"Let's not be silly Michael … or maudlin. What you got was noticed, that's all."

I needed to get away – even five minutes – just to be free of her haggard face before I jumped across the table and broke that turkey neck. Taking a deep breath, I stood.

"Amanda, I need a clean shirt."

"Upstairs, second door on the right, Harry's things are there, help yourself."

I had to ask,

"Don't you feel anything for Harry, I mean … any grief, or regret?"

She was mid-bite and put up a hand to catch a crumb.

"No, no, I can't really say that I do. The funeral's on Thursday, your first public appearance as family patriarch. Will you be assuming the position?"

"Maybe it's what I do best."

Upstairs, I flung open a wardrobe and a line of safari suits saluted me.

"Jesus," I said, and closed it.

I went through a range of presses and found a dozen Krugerrands. Put them in my pocket and selected a dark Argyll sweater. The price tag still on it. In a corner was a heavy sealed envelope so I tore it open.

A gun fell to the floor with a leaflet explaining how to use and maintain it, plus ammunition. I read the instructions carefully and slowly before I touched it. According to what I read, it was a .45 calibre automatic, as used by the military. It didn't say which particular military but I thought it fair to assume a kick-ass outfit. The style of the instructions and description were of the gung-ho variety – along the lines of

"You now hold in your hand
one of the most efficient
deterrents as utilized by
today's modern soldier."

Like the ads you found in *Playboy,* appealing to the arrogant asshole you wished to be.

I picked it up and my life changed. In that spasm of time I went from confusion to absolute clarity. I could understand why it was called an equalizer and why people went apeshit with them. Right then and there, I wanted to shoot someone, anyone. It felt electric in my hand, it felt home.

I tucked it in the back of my waistband as I'd seen on *The Professionals* and realized I was the American Dream:

white,
rich,
single-ish.

And even better, I already had a body count, not major league, not yet, but hell, the day was young and spring was coming. I started down the stairs, shouted,

"Amanda ... Consuela ... Come and see what Daddy's found."